Slam Dunk
Sporting Pride #6
Charity Parkerson

Punk & Sissy Publications

Copyright

—Warning: This book is intended for readers over the age of 18. Some of my books contain allusions to past abuse and trauma.

Contents

Introduction

DESPITE HIS FAME, JATHAN'S personal life is pretty bland. He's always the friend on the outside looking in. Quince sees him.

With the season coming to a close, Jathan is coming into that six-month season of his life every year where boredom strikes. His circle is filled with people just as famous as he is, and maybe that's the problem. He only has one friend who genuinely likes him, and he just got married. This year, Jathan has to get out there and meet more people with

1

similar interests. Unfortunately, he's kind of awkward.

Since Jathan started visiting the ranch to spend time with Quince's boss's new husband, Quince hasn't looked away. Jathan is tall, gorgeous, and funny. Only recently has he noticed Quince at all. Now Quince is fully obsessed with someone he can't have. There's too much standing between them—mostly Quince and all the things he can't say. It's an issue.

Slam Dunk is the sixth book in Charity Parkerson's Sporting Pride series. These are sports-related romances, following men who find love while navigating high-profile careers. These are best enjoyed when read in order.

Chapter One

AN ELBOW TO THE ribs was always a fun time. Jathan got it, though. It was the playoffs, and the other team was losing. That always made for dirty plays. Still, Jathan felt an odd mixture of relief and sadness when the buzzer sounded. Soon, this would be over. No matter how far they went this year, it always ended. People hugged and pulled elaborate handshakes. They were just games away from going to the conference finals. It was surreal. Even though it wasn't his first time making it this far, he still felt crazy proud of this team. It was definitely a brotherhood... on the court. As soon as the handshakes passed, everyone returned to their worlds, where they would celebrate with their group. He knew why he wasn't truly part of any clique. No one said it, though. He was too talented to slur. As soon as that ended, though, Jathan already knew what the headlines would look like.

Jathan turned in a circle, eyeing the building he had called home for the last nine years. He had lasted longer than at least seventy-five percent of players in the league. The Fireballs had picked him up at eighteen and he had worked his ass off for them in every sense. The pay matched, though. Still, in his heart of hearts, he knew he was only a few short years away from the end.

A familiar form in a cowboy hat moved through the floor seats toward the end of the aisle. Happiness soared through Jathan.

He let out a loud whistle. "Quince!" Nothing. Jathan panicked a little. He couldn't let him get away. A ball boy was nearby, working. Jathan caught his eye and waved for a ball. The guy tossed it his way.

Thankfully, Jathan was known for his accuracy. He chucked the ball into the crowd, hitting Quince square in the back. Quince turned, looking confused as hell.

Jathan bit back a laugh as he threw his hands up. "Are you really going to leave without even saying hi?" Jathan shouted the question, ensuring he was heard.

Quince looked around, obviously irritated by the slow-moving crowd. Giving up, he started climbing over chairs and making his way toward the court. A security guard tried to stop him.

Jathan let out another sharp whistle. The security guard turned. "He's with me."

With a nod, he stepped aside and let Quince dip into the crowd on the court. Jathan never lost sight of him. Not only was Quince almost as tall as Jathan, but his cowboy hat also stood out. Finally, sexy steel-colored eyes were on him. Quince's too-gorgeous smile was there. "Hey. I didn't really think I'd get to say hi. I just figured I'd let you know next time you're out at the ranch that I saw the game."

Jathan shook his head. "Let me see your phone."

Quince pulled it from his pocket without question. He unlocked it before passing it along.

Jathan pulled up his contacts and added his information. "I'm adding my number. Next time, text me before the game." He passed it back.

Their fingers brushed. Their gazes held. It was always like this. Quince was the foreman at Jathan's best friend's ranch. Since Jathan spent a lot of time with Artem, he ran across Quince just as often. Truthfully, he deliberately stepped into his path every chance he got. The guy was solid muscle. Wide chest and cut jaw. He should be on the cover of those rugged cowboy romance books. Jathan was all the way into him, but he honestly had no clue if the guy had any interest in men. He fit the straight stereotype.

"What are you doing for the rest of the night?"

Quince toyed with his phone, shifting it from one hand to the other. "Nothing, really."

"I'm parked on the players' level in the garage. Section D. Meet me at my car. Let's go do something."

Quince gave him a nod. "Sounds good."

He turned, as if trying to figure out how to get there.

Jathan touched his bicep to get his attention. The hard muscle beneath his hand nearly took him out. He pointed toward a nearby door. "Go through there. That's the players' tunnel. There's an elevator to the right. It'll take you straight to the garage. It only goes to one floor."

Quince's beautiful eyes focused on him again. "Thanks. See you in a few."

Jathan nodded while trying to hold on to his pride. "See you."

He watched the perfect ass in form-fitting jeans every step he took to the door. Damn. He was breathtaking. Jathan had no idea where they would go. He still couldn't get there fast enough.

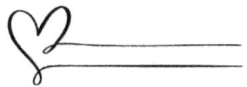

Since Jathan was often at the ranch, Quince spotted Jathan's Hummer immediately. Even if Jathan hadn't told him this was the players' garage, Quince would have known it. The multimillion-dollar cars lining the garage were the first giveaway. The second was when various players began pouring from the elevator. Quince leaned against the passenger side door of Jathan's car and tried to look as if he belonged. That also meant he couldn't show his ass, asking for selfies and autographs. He simply nodded as some of the most famous names in modern-day basketball walked past him.

Finally, the third wave of players included Jathan. Quince automatically smiled at the sight of him. He always caught himself wearing a huge grin when Jathan was around.

Jathan stumbled over nothing as he switched his bag from one hand to the other. He glanced behind him as if trying to figure out what had grabbed his foot. Quince couldn't stop smiling. It was just his big-ass feet and lanky body. He was like a giraffe. When he looked up, he caught Quince staring.

Quince dipped his chin in greeting—like they hadn't seen each other already tonight.

"Sorry it took so long. There're always after game interviews and whatnot. I didn't think about that when I asked you to wait, but I'm glad I did."

The doors of his SUV unlocked.

Jathan motioned toward it. "Get in."

Quince didn't even question where they were going. He didn't care. He was probably one of Jathan's biggest fans. Of course, he would drop dead before he said that. Quince wasn't that guy. He was a country boy all the way to his heart. Quince had grown up on a ranch and he would die on one. This was just some sort of crazy slice out of time. He didn't imagine people like Jathan kept friends like him.

He put on his seatbelt while Jathan dumped his bag on the backseat. He watched as he climbed behind the wheel. Even the large vehicle seemed small for his long legs. Quince wasn't short. In fact, he was six-six and used to hovering over everyone. Jathan was still taller.

"Where are we headed?"

Jathan laughed at the question. "Honestly, I hoped you had an idea. I'm kind of boring."

Like always, Jathan had him smiling. "What are you talking about? I barely leave the ranch. How would I know what to do?"

Jathan's wide grin made him look like a guy who was just nice as hell, and he was. That was what Quince couldn't get over. "Damn. Um, have you eaten?"

Quince shook his head. "I'd planned to grab something on the way home."

"Good." Jathan pulled from the parking spot he was backed into. "I'm starved."

"I'll bet after that game."

Jathan cocked his head and looked thoughtful. "Truthfully, I don't think I was as good as I could've been tonight. We won, but I can't start slipping now."

"Congratulations on that win, by the way. I think you did great." A thought occurred to him. "I'm surprised you're not out with your teammates, celebrating."

"I'm gay."

That wasn't a surprise to Quince. He had obsessively researched everything about Jathan, and Jathan's best friend was gay. That didn't necessarily mean anything. Still, Quince knew that already.

Thankfully, Jathan kept talking and spared him from responding. "It shouldn't matter, and it doesn't matter when we're on the court. But no one wants to be seen with me in any other setting. Not really. That might make people think they're gay too and God forbid, right?" Jathan laughed. It was an awkward sound—like he expected the worst from Quince now.

Even though Jathan watched the road, Quince shrugged. "Their loss, then. Where would you like to eat?"

"Oh." Jathan laughed again. He was hilariously artless. It was like he didn't know he was a household name. "I really just started driving with no plan."

He had to know. "Where would you have gone if I hadn't said anything?"

Jathan glanced around, as if he had no clue where he was. "My house probably. That's where muscle memory had me headed."

Quince shrugged. "I'd say, let's just do that, then. We can grab something through a drive-thru. But you're used to people not wanting to be seen with you. You should get to go out and celebrate properly. What would you be doing right now if you were included?"

"Everyone always goes to Area 9 to party. It's this really pretentious nightclub. Honestly, unless that's what you'd prefer to do, I'm not big on that sort of thing. I can't dance. I don't drink." He looked thoughtful for a moment. "You know, it's possible that's why no one really invites me to things." A bark of laughter burst from him. "Oh, well. How about Steakhouse 7?"

That place was super expensive. Quince never went there for that reason. He could afford it. Tip paid him well, but he just couldn't convince himself to pay over a hundred dollars for one meal.

"I'm paying, by the way," Jathan tacked on.

"You don't have to do that."

"I asked you to do something. That means I pay. Now, you're not a vegetarian or anything, right? If so, I can pick something different." He sounded unsure—like maybe he insulted Quince with the idea of eating meat.

"Nah. Steakhouse 7 is great."

Jathan flashed him a goofy smile that did something to Quince's chest. He already didn't want the night to end.

Chapter Two

THROUGHOUT DINNER, JATHAN TALKED too much. To be fair, he didn't get to talk to people often, except his mom—who he talked to every day. Also, to be honest, he was a talker. He had definitely gotten into trouble every day at school because he couldn't be quiet. Not only did Quince seem unbothered, but he also came home with Jathan.

They climbed from Jathan's Hummer in his garage. His car collection sat on one side of the building while his pottery studio was on the other. It had expanded significantly. He had recently bought twice the equipment and supplies so he could teach Artem. It was nice having someone to share his hobbies with.

Quince nodded toward a nearby sports car. "There's no way you can drive that at your height."

Jathan headed for his Bugatti Chiron. "I just fit, but I can. The passenger seat gives a hair more room. But I think, since you're maybe two inches shorter than me, my seat settings would work even better for you." He opened the driver's side door.

Quince took off his cowboy hat and looked inside. Jathan couldn't look at anything but him. "This is gorgeous. Tip has all the money, but he's not a big car-collecting type of guy. He's addicted to buying land."

"Yeah, he's smarter than me. He's actually making an investment." Jathan never hesitated to be honest about himself. He had spoiled himself for a little while. Jathan had calmed down in the last few years. He understood his money had to last him for the rest of his life.

"Climb in. The getting out is the hardest part."

Quince looked nervous. "Nah. My boots always have some mud somewhere on them. I don't want to get your car dirty."

Jathan shook his head. "I'm not worried about that. What's the point of owning a car if you don't enjoy it? Come on." He motioned again toward the driver's side. Jathan circled the car and climbed into the passenger seat. He settled in to wait.

Finally, Quince eased behind the wheel. "Damn. There really is more room than it seems. I think if you were two inches taller, it'd be impossible for you to drive."

"Agreed. Shut the door. Let's go for a ride."

Quince's panicked gaze shot his way. "No way in hell I'm driving a three-million-dollar car. I don't even know what that kind of money looks like."

"Actually, this version is ten million, but it's cool. Come on. It's insured. You can drive like a granny, if you want. You know you want to." Jathan used his best cajoling voice.

Quince stared straight ahead for a moment.

Jathan held his breath.

Quince shut his door.

With a hyena-sounding laugh, Jathan strapped in before showing Quince how to do the same.

Quince glanced in the mirror and then looked behind him. "How do you open the garage?"

"Just start inching back. It'll open."

Quince did as instructed. He looked nervous as hell. Jathan's eyes refused to budge from him. He forced them away. Quince was already uncomfortable. Jathan didn't want to make it worse. Quince genuinely drove like an elderly person for one spin around the block before returning to the garage. The door opened automatically again as they approached. When Quince killed the engine, he released a breath so hard, Jathan wondered if he had been holding the air in his lungs the entire time.

"Whee!"

At Jathan's unexpected squeal of delight, Quince burst out laughing. His eyes swam with happiness. "You're one of a kind. You know that, right?"

Quince's claim had a pain stabbing Jathan right in the chest. He liked Quince too much. He was already getting too attached for having no idea if Quince would want to do this again.

"Same. Do you want to drive any of the rest of these cars?"

Quince didn't even look. He pulled a pitiful face. "Please don't ever make me do that again."

"Don't worry. I promise I'll never hit you with peer pressure again." With a laugh, Jathan jumped from the car. "Come on. Let's see what else we can play with." Jathan bit his bottom lip as he headed for the door. He was having the greatest time. Quince had to stay.

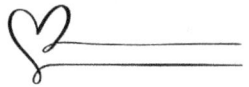

Quince drove home, smiling. He couldn't force the grin away. The night had been the most fun he'd had in years. A notification popped up on the dashboard's infotainment system. The flash caught his eyes.

"Siri, read the last text to me."

"Carey says, do you want to play? Smiley face. Wink. Do you want to respond?"

His mood immediately crashed. "No." The night had been so damn good. Another flash had Quince ready to leap from the vehicle and end it all.

"Siri, read the last text to me."

"Carey says you're not still angry, are you? You know we have a good time. Would you like to respond?"

"Yes. Go fuck yourself."

"You said, go fuck yourself. Send it?"

"Yes."

"Done."

The flash struck again. "Oh, for fuck's sake. Siri, read the last text to me."

"Jathan says, I had a nice time. Maybe we could do it again sometime. Would you like to respond?"

A smile exploded across his face. "Yes. Tonight was a blast. Just say when and where and I'm there."

"You said, tonight was a blast. Just say when and where and I'm there. Send it?"

"Yes."

"Done."

The music resumed. It was an old love song Quince had always loved. He turned the sound up and sang along. His mood was officially restored after Jathan's text. The drive out to the ranch was nothing but quiet. The darkness was only broken by Quince's presence. He felt at peace in a way he hadn't in a long time. The way he felt since walking away from Carey made him realize how much he wasn't cut out for relationships. He hated lying and drama. Quince couldn't stand the head games and questioning every little word and action. He was better off alone. Obviously, he would miss the sex. But he didn't yet, and the headache he avoided without it was worth every unquenched desire. Having a new friend was better. Quince chuckled. He didn't even care he was alone. Quince laughed aloud. He was horrified every time he thought about the way he had creeped around that block like a teen driving for the first time. Jathan hadn't once made fun of him the way every other guy he knew would have done. Quince laughed harder as he pictured Jathan, eyes swimming with humor while squealing, "Whee!" Quince swiped his eyes. God. The guy was unintentionally hilarious. It had been a nice night.

When Jathan had dropped Quince back at his truck, he had given Quince a hug. That had been nice too. He missed those kinds of friendships. Before walking away from everything twelve years ago, Quince had several friends he hung out with on the weekends—guys he could call if he needed a hand working on his truck or something. Now he lived out in the middle of nowhere and had no one. He had gotten used to doing things like going to basketball games alone. Fuck. That ticket tonight had been a goddamn fortune. A playoff game just rows from the court. That had been a huge score, but it cost him way more than he would ever admit. Right now, it looked like the best purchase he had made in a long time. Never in a million years had he expected Jathan would spot him and pull him from the crowd. Damn. He was a great guy. It was no wonder Artem always made time for him. Of course, considering how out of this world Artem was, he shouldn't have been surprised by Jathan. All it took to judge a man's character was to take a look at his friends. Like always found like. Quince wished he had heeded that advice more in his younger years.

His house came into view. A wave of unexpected exhaustion hit. It had been a long day with too much adrenaline. Maybe he should jump online and see if there was any chance of landing a ticket to the next game. Damn. It would be in Arlington on their court. Maybe the game after that, then. He hoped like hell the Fireballs went all the way this year. The team had been close now for several years. Jathan deserved to win that championship title again. He was incredible on the court.

Quince tossed his keys on the coffee table. He grabbed a drink from the fridge. After downing his water, he headed for the bathroom. He needed a shower. Tomorrow morning would come early. Unfortunately, this ranch didn't run itself. The guys were all pretty good about knowing their roles for the day, but if he slacked, they would. Plus, he needed to check all the fencing. They had a sheep a neighbor had brought back three times now. Quince had to figure out how in the hell it kept getting out.

He got the shower going and stripped. From nowhere, Quince caught himself eyeing his body. He didn't think he looked too bad for forty. Other than a few scars here and there—some worse than others—he had held up well. Not that it mattered. Quince stepped beneath the water. He was done with anything even vaguely resembling a relationship. That meant one-night stands too. No one ever really meant one night, and he was tired. Quince turned his face up and let the hot water run through his hair. He grabbed the shampoo and lathered it through, massaging his scalp. With his eyes closed, his body betrayed him. The water streaming down his skin made itself known. He became hyperaware of every inch of his skin. His cock hardened. Quince took a breath. He tried not to think about anything the least bit sexual. It didn't help. Apparently, his body was just determined tonight. With an aggravated sigh, Quince palmed his erection. He kept his eyes closed as he stroked. Ruthlessly, he kept his mind blank. He didn't want anyone sneaking in and making him doubt his ability to stay single. His lips parted as pressure climbed up his shaft. He was close. Quince didn't need anyone. He could blow right here and be done with this bullshit. The closer he came to orgasm, the dirtier his mind turned. It was out of his control. Images rolled through his mind. He tried focusing on celebrities or random faces he had seen in his dreams. Pleasure pressed against his crown, begging to be set free. Quince stroked faster. His ragged breathing filled the shower. The person on their knees in his mind transformed. Quince stared down at Jathan, looking like a man who loved sucking cock. He blew so hard and fast, his knees nearly buckled. Quince whined as he stroked his way through the waves. Then the world snapped back into focus.

Quince stared at the shower wall. He fought to keep his mind quiet. Quince was scared to think. Why had that happened? He felt a little sick. What was wrong with him? Why had things been so goddamn weird lately? Maybe he was going through a mid-life crisis. That had to be it. Quince had done a lot of wild things in his life, but he had never really wanted a dude. He practically felt his dad rolling over in his grave and the man wasn't even dead yet. Not since he was a teenager had Quince even had thoughts like that. Maybe he shouldn't hang out with Jathan again after all. He wasn't that guy. Yeah. This had been a one and done. Quince wasn't gay. He couldn't be.

Chapter Three

EVEN THOUGH HE WAS normally an upbeat person, Jathan's mood was complete shit. They'd lost their game in Arlington. While they still had a chance, they had to win the next home game. His mom had been sick with the flu throughout the playoffs and hadn't made it to a single game, so there really had been no one there supporting him. It was tough being the outsider. Everyone had family or friends at their biggest games. Jathan had given his tickets away since he had no one else with Artem and Tip in Arizona looking at land.

He had really hoped his mom would be well enough for tomorrow's game, but she still had a super-high fever. Jathan tried hard not to be upset since no one was more devastated than her. Thankfully, Artem and Tip were back in town, so he didn't have to look pathetic by giving his tickets away to another player again. Of course, that still hinged on the pair being able to go.

As he pulled into Artem's driveway, he spotted Quince in the barn. An idea hit. Quince had seemed thrilled to be at his game. Court-side might make his day. He hadn't said anything to Artem yet. There was no reason Jathan couldn't give Quince the tickets and he could decide who to take. There was also a possibility Quince wasn't interested. Jathan had to admit he had kind of hoped to hear from Quince after hitting it off the way they had. At least he had thought they'd hit it off. Other than responding to his text directly after their night together, there had been nothing but radio silence. That was pretty typical, though. Jathan always liked people better than they liked him. He wasn't sure where he went wrong. Maybe he was too weird or too enthusiastic. It was possible he tried too hard. No matter the reason, it hurt his chest to constantly be rejected. Meeting Artem was the first time in his life he'd had an immediate connection that was reciprocated. He just wasn't that important to people off the court.

Jathan parked in his usual spot and grabbed his things. He plastered a bright smile on his face and dipped into the barn. He found Quince mucking out stalls.

"Hey."

Quince glanced over his shoulder. "Hey."

Jathan tried to read his tone but couldn't. "What have you been up to?"

"Working." This time, Quince didn't bother looking at him.

Okay. He was definitely reading too much into every word now. There was an unwanted vibe he couldn't shake. "Oh. Well, I'm here to paint with Artem. I just wanted to dip in here and ask if you'd be interested in goin—"

"I'm not gay." Quince said the words, cutting him off sharply—like he meant that shit.

"Okay. What?" Jathan was beyond confused. Had he felt something the other night? Yes. Did he expect anything more than friendship? No. He never assumed.

Quince held his stare. There was no friendship in his eyes. "I'm not gay."

Yeah. Jathan was pissed. He was also hurt. But rejection was a familiar feeling for him.

He stiffened his spine. "Okay. I don't know what in the fuck that has to do with me. I just came in here to see if you wanted court seats for tomorrow night's game, but never mind. You obviously can't accept anything from a gay man. I might be contagious." Jathan walked away and headed for the door. He couldn't breathe, but he kept going. It took too long for Artem to answer. Jathan didn't think he would survive much longer.

Artem was all smiles. "Hey. I was just setting things up."

He really hoped his smile wasn't as brittle as it felt. "Hey. Sorry. I can't stay. My mom just called as I pulled in and she needs some help today. But can I please throw myself on your mercy?" He pulled the tickets from his back pocket. "Will you please come to my game tomorrow night? I haven't had anyone on the sidelines since game one. It's—"

"Of course." Artem didn't hesitate to take the tickets while stopping Jathan from having to humble himself even more. "I'd love to be there. Why didn't you say something before I went out of town? I would've stayed so you'd have someone."

Jathan still couldn't breathe properly. "I had high hopes Mom would make it, but she's had the flu. She's not really getting better."

Artem pulled a face. "Be careful visiting her, then. It's going around hard right now. You don't want to get knocked out of the game. I know how much it means to you."

Jathan kept nodding. That was exactly why his mom had told him to stay away.

Artem's gaze moved over his face. "Are you okay? What else is going on?"

Jathan tried harder to smile. "I'm good. Just under a lot of pressure and stress right now.

I really needed this day with you today, but it's my mom."

Artem closed the distance between them and hugged him. "Can I come to you? We can work on pottery later. Never mind. I'm not asking. I'll be at your place at six with dinner and we can stay up all night talking. Tip can live without me for one night."

He was Jathan's best friend for a reason. Artem was always there. He was all Jathan needed. Fuck Quince. "Sounds great. I'd love that, actually."

Artem took a step back. "I'll be there. Okay? I love you."

The pressure eased in Jathan's chest. "I love you too. See you in a few hours."

Artem nodded. "Be careful on the drive home."

Jathan kissed Artem's cheek. "I will." He turned and jogged down the front steps. Jathan walked with purpose. He couldn't get out of there fast enough.

When he reached his SUV, Quince stepped from the barn. "Can we talk?"

Jathan leveled his most hate-filled look at Quince. "No. You don't have shit to say to me." He climbed inside his Hummer and backed from the driveway without looking back. Quince had already said all Jathan needed to hear. There was no need for them to ever talk again.

In all his years, Quince had never felt worse. Honest to God, he had no idea why he had done that. That wasn't true. When he had seen Jathan's Hummer pull into the driveway, his reaction had scared the fuck out of him. He had been thrilled... and hungry. Fuck. His. Life. He wanted Jathan. Once, when he was a teen, a friend had spent the night and come onto him in the middle of the night. Quince hadn't said no. That was the first and only time he had done anything with a guy. They had never spoken again. Quince hadn't thought anything about it. He had been in those years where he got hard rubbing against his jeans the wrong way. Of course, he had been down to get off any way he could.

This was different. He was the one who wanted something. It had him fucked up. Where was he supposed to go with that? Goddamn it. He'd had the best time with Jathan. Too many things were becoming clearer. All the times he had watched Jathan when he had been there with Artem. He hadn't fully realized that infatuation hadn't been about Jathan being his favorite basketball player. He had wanted to get closer to Jathan. Quince always fought to find reasons to be near him. He got hit with all that at once and then Jathan had been there—all smiles and sunshine. Quince's shoulders fell. He was a pussy. No more or less. He was a coward.

Darkness fell. Quince's muscles screamed. He had worked himself to death in punishment. Plus, he wanted to fall into bed and pass out at the end of the day. Quince couldn't go to bed with Jathan's hurt expression stuck in his head. And how fucking vain was he, thinking Jathan could actually want him? Like just because the guy was gay, he wanted every guy he was nice to. Quince moved to a nearby bale of hay and sat. What was wrong with him? That should have been his first thought. Quince was forty, for fuck's sake. Jathan was twenty-seven, gorgeous, and famous. Rich. Quince was absolutely nobody. He was an idiot.

"I thought I saw you moving around out here." Tip's voice pulled Quince from his thoughts.

He focused on the polished retired soccer player who hired him twelve years ago. They were both older. Hell, that wasn't hard for Tip. At the time, Quince had thought he was taking a huge risk on a nineteen-year-old newly minted millionaire. Little had he known Tip would turn out to have an older and wiser soul than anyone alive. He had been good to Quince. They were friends.

"Hey. Yeah. I had a lot to catch up on. Two of the guys are out with the flu."

Tip nodded. His hazel eyes always looked too serious. "It's odd how hard that virus has hit this year. I didn't think people really caught that this time of year, but what do I know?"

A lot, in Quince's opinion. He was one of the smartest people Quince knew. Tip had taken his first million and turned it into hundreds of millions. In some ways, he was a bit of a genius.

"Yeah. I'm trying my best to avoid that shit."

With his hands in his pockets, Tip turned in a circle, eyeing everything. Quince knew what he saw. The barn was spotless. Quince had been serious about killing himself.

"Jathan's mom has been down for over a week now and still has a fever. She's missed all this set of playoff games. I gather he's been a little down about no one coming to cheer him on."

Fuck. It just kept getting worse. "I went the other night. It cost a goddamn arm and a leg."

Tip focused on him. He held Quince's stare. "I heard."

Oh no. Tip knew, and he wasn't happy. Quince refused to say anything and incriminate himself. "Where's Artem tonight? It's not like you to hang around out here?"

Tip paced away. He moved to pet Artem's horse, Ginger. "He went to spend the night with Jathan and get wine drunk. You've worked for me a long time."

It really was as bad as Quince suspected. He couldn't lose this job. This was his home. He literally lived on property and had made this job his life. "Twelve years."

"In all those years, I never once suspected I'd hired a homophobe. I'll give you that."

Yep. He was fucked. "You didn't."

Tip looked his way and held Quince's stare.

Quince refused to look away. "You didn't."

Tip chose a spot and sat across from him. "Then what in the fuck is going in, because I got to tell you, Quince, Jathan is one of the nicest people on the planet. Being mean to him is like kicking a puppy. Why in the fuck would you say that shit to him?"

Quince took a breath. He didn't know where to start.

Tip obviously took his hesitation as him searching for a lie. "I need you to be honest with me. If Jathan feels like he can't come here, then I'll be dealing with more of this—sleeping alone. I much prefer Jathan come to Artem. If he won't because of you, then I have some thinking to do."

There it was. His job was on the line. Quince couldn't be a bitch. "I like him."

Tip looked as if he waited for more, and it hit Quince. He didn't know what Quince meant.

"I like him, like him."

Tip sat back. "Huh. Okay. Were you one of those kids that pulled people's hair when you had a crush?"

Despite the seriousness of the situation, Quince laughed. "No. Believe it or not, I didn't have much interest in anyone until I was like sixteen. But no, I'm not the type to act like this. I've never dated a guy. This has got me a little fucked up, but I tried to talk to him again before he left, so I could apologize and explain. He wouldn't talk to me. Not that I know if I can explain what even I don't understand." Quince swiped his hand over his face. Aggravation rose inside him, making everything feel overwhelming and pissing him off. "And you know what, if I had anywhere else to go, I'd walk away from this job right now. I've worked my ass off for you for twelve years and you're really ready to fire me over one thing. That's bullshit. I thought we were friends."

"I didn't say that. In fact, I can't think of many things you could do to make me fire you. This is your home. You're more than a friend. You're like family to me. I only meant I might have to find a way to guarantee you're nowhere nearby when Jathan stops by."

Quince's shoulders dropped. It had truly been the worst day. "I really don't know how to fix this. There's a reason I live out here and barely have anything to do with anyone. I'm not good at this part of life. Part of me thinks that's exactly what I should do. I should just make myself scarce when he comes to visit and let it be. The rest of me really wants to say I'm sorry."

"Text him."

Quince blinked. He felt a little stupid. Jathan's number was in his phone. Texting was so much easier than talking. He could just text him. "Yeah. Okay. I'll try. Hopefully, he'll accept my apology, and—at the very least—be okay with coming back out here for Artem."

Tip stood. "I'll leave you to do that. No doubt Artem will let me know how it goes."

A snort burst from Quince. "I'm sure."

"Good luck." Tip flashed him a smile and headed out, leaving Quince to figure it out.

Quince pulled out his phone and stared at Jathan's name. He didn't want to do this here. Quince made his way to his truck and quickly drove around the property to his place. Once there, he decided to shower first. Only when he couldn't avoid it any longer did Quince start typing.

Quince: *So, turns out I might be a little gay. Since the other night, I've had thoughts about you I've never had about a guy. Too late, I realized how incredibly ridiculous my reaction was to realizing how you make me feel. I feel so dumb. First off, you didn't deserve any of that shit and I'm sorry. No excuses. I'm just sorry. Secondly, how stupid am I thinking someone like you would even think about someone like me in that light? I can't fucking believe I automatically acted like you'd want me just because you were nice to me. Jesus. The more I type, the more I realize you shouldn't ever talk to me again.*

I deserve your hatred. Before you block my number, just let me say I'm sorry. Being with you was the most fun I've had in well over a decade. I'm fully aware this is my loss. Good luck with the rest of the playoffs and have a great life, I guess.

Quince read the text four times before hitting send. He knew he had said too much, but he also couldn't think of what to cut out. Jathan deserved a thousand-word essay on how much Quince regretted losing a friend. If he had one defense, it was that he had always been a terrible judge of character. It made sense he would ruin something good.

Quince headed for the bedroom. He plugged his phone in and set it on the bedside table before he stripped down to his underwear. After climbing into bed, he stared at the ceiling. Maybe he should have said more. He could have confessed to a million things. Nothing changed anything, though. He'd had a shot at some level of happiness and blown it. Maybe he should take Carey back after all. He couldn't say she was wrong for cheating on him. What did he have to offer at the end of the day? Nothing.

His phone buzzed.

Quince's gaze slid toward the device. A loud, annoyed sigh burst from Quince. It was always like conjuring up the devil with Carey. He had dumped her a million times and taken her back every time, so it was fair for her to think he would do it again. It wasn't like he felt anything for her anyhow beyond the fact that she was familiar. She was someone he didn't have to work for. He snagged the phone. In no universe did he expect to see Jathan's name, but there it was. His hands shook as he opened the message.

Jathan: *Can I call?*

Well, shit. So much for texting being easier.

Quince: *Yes*.

His phone rang almost immediately. He took a steadying breath before answering. "Hello?"

"Hey."

"Hey."

Silence dragged between them. Still, Quince felt better knowing Jathan was on the other end of the line.

"So, I'm a little drunk. I apologize now if I say anything totally dumb."

A smile exploded across Quince's face. "I kind of like that about you. Everyone is pretty serious around me all the time. I thought you didn't drink."

"I don't. It didn't take much to get me here." Jathan paused. He heard Jathan blow out a sigh. "So here's the thing. When I asked you to dinner the other night, I really kind of meant the offer as a date. But then I got worried you didn't see it that way, so I decided to pull back and just accept whatever because I really don't have any friends, so that was good too. Does that make any sense, or am I just rambling? I feel like I'm rambling."

Just like that night, Quince hadn't stopped grinning like an idiot from the moment Jathan started talking. "I get what you're saying. When I left, I couldn't stop smiling, thinking about how much fun I had and how great you are. I don't really have friends either, so I was ridiculously excited. But then I started looking way too closely at things and I realized I wanted more. Then I panicked, and I always fuck things up when that happens. I guess my point is, I genuinely like you a lot. If we can be friends, then I really want that."

"What if I want more?"

God. He would not be a fucking coward and regret it for the rest of his life. "Then I really want that too, but I'll take whichever you choose because I was serious. I've never been happier than I was the other night. You're really amazing. I loved spending time with you."

Another bout of silence fell between them. He might have thought their call had dropped if he didn't hear Jathan moving around.

"So, what are you wearing?"

A bark of laughter burst from Quince. Lord, he was so much fun. "Sorry. I just got a sudden image of Artem sitting there, listening in horror."

Jathan laughed. It was a sexy sound. "Nah. I ended up drinking his wine. Since he was sober when I got your text, he decided to go home. I'm surprised he lasted as long as he did. He wouldn't do well sleeping away from Tip."

It was a little horrific thinking about Artem reading his text alongside Jathan, but whatever. At this point, he had already humiliated himself all over the place. "Yeah. Even if he'd gotten drunk, Tip probably would've come to get him. He doesn't like to share."

A sexy chuckle caressed his ear through the phone. "You never said what you're wearing. Was that intentional?"

Damn. Now that he had Jathan talking sexy in his ear, things didn't feel that strange after all. He was an adult. Quince wanted what he wanted. He wouldn't back down. "No. I just got into bed before I got your text, so I'm in my underwear."

"Wow. You meant it. You're really willing to go past friendship."

Quince smirked. Now he felt like the man he truly was. He wasn't weak. "If you'll actually go for someone old like me, then hell yeah. What are you wearing?"

Jathan's laughter was everything. "Sadly, I'm fully dressed. The room is spinning quite a bit. I really hate drinking."

"Keep one foot on the floor."

"Solid advice." Jathan sounded tired. "I gave my court-side tickets to Artem and Tip."

"How are you getting to the game?"

"It's not that far, so I'm driving."

Quince felt good on the inside. Warm. He didn't care about any fucking tickets. "Then you can celebrate with me after you win."

"I'd like that."

"It's sounds like you're falling asleep on me."

"That sounds nice." He honestly sounded half asleep. "You have a great chest. I bet it makes an amazing pillow."

"You should find out sometime. Right now, you need to go to bed before you pass out. We can talk tomorrow." When Jathan was sober. He hoped Jathan remembered this and didn't wake up still finished with him.

"Okay. Quince?"

Quince smiled. It sounded in the voice. "Yeah?"

"I'm glad you're still my friend."

He still hoped to be more. "Me too."

"Goodnight."

Quince really didn't want to hang up. "Goodnight." With nothing left to do, Quince hit end. For much longer than he cared to admit, Quince held his phone and stared at the ceiling. It had been a day. For the first time in a long time, he couldn't wait to see what happened tomorrow.

Chapter Four

THE SCREECH OF RUBBER soles on the polished floor and the smell of the game were as familiar to Jathan as breathing. Each time he spotted Artem cheering for him, his chest warmed. He felt a hell of a lot better tonight. His head was fully in the game. This time, when the buzzer sounded on their win, Jathan knew they would go all the way. He felt it in his bones.

Artem jumped up and down, eagerly accepting his sweaty hug. Adrenaline pumped so hard through his veins, he couldn't retain anything he saw or heard.

Life just passed in some odd sort of surreality. He chatted, smiled, hugged, and gave interviews. Everything moved in a blur. He didn't feel any sense of reality return until he headed for the elevator with his bag tossed over his shoulder and scrolled through his phone. The usual congratulatory texts from his mom waited along with a text from Quince.

Quince: *I'll be waiting at your place with food by the time you get there.*

A smile exploded across Jathan's face. He hadn't known if he would hear from Quince. Their drunken conversation—on his side—was a bit of a blur, but Jathan recalled enough. He wanted to see him. Jathan needed to know where this was headed. For once, he felt hopeful about the future in some way other than his career. He absolutely broke the speed limit the entire way home, making record time.

Sure enough, Quince sat in his truck in the driveway. Jathan smiled so hard, he probably looked like a crazy person. The garage door opened. Jathan slowed as he passed and waved for Quince to follow him inside. There was plenty of room inside for him to park. Obviously catching his drift, Quince pulled in next to him. The garage door slid closed behind them, shutting them away from the world.

Quince jumped from the truck, carrying bags of food. He was all smiles. "You fucking did it. I knew you would. You're amazing."

It felt beyond fantastic having Quince praise him. He was on top of the world. "One more game to the finals."

"You'll get there. I feel it."

For a moment, they simply stared at each other. Jathan had to break the spell. "We should head inside. Whatever you brought smells delicious."

"It's just like hamburgers and fries. I was in a hurry to see you."

He hadn't felt this much hope in a long time. Jathan motioned for Quince to follow and headed inside. He grabbed two drinks from the fridge and got them set up in the living room.

"It's funny. You have this huge house with a perfectly decorated dining room and you eat on the couch."

Jathan hadn't even thought. He just sat where he always did. "We can move to the dining room, if you'd like. I didn't think about how you'd be most comfortable."

Quince shook his head. "I eat while sitting on the couch too. You just seem like someone who would care if food got spilled on their sofa."

He had no idea what that meant, but he still laughed. "No. It can be cleaned. What I can't stand is sitting by myself in the dining room and the silence, eating alone. At least here, the TV keeps me company."

Quince nodded. "I get it. How's your mom?" He ate and held Jathan's stare as he waited for Jathan to answer.

"She thinks her fever finally broke this morning. Since this game won us home advantage, she plans to be at the next one. That leaves an extra seat." He dug into his food.

"You don't want to give that to another family member?"

Jathan shook his head as he swallowed his bite. "There's no one else. It's just Mom and me."

"I'd be honored to sit with your mom, then."

There was so much happiness swelling in his chest. He ate too fast. Jathan really was starved after games. "What about your family? What are they like?" Before Quince could answer, Jathan held up one finger. "I know I'm weird, but I'll have to listen from down here." He pushed the coffee table aside and settled on the floor. Flat on his back, he propped his feet on the couch, trying to alleviate some of the pressure on his lower spine. "Okay. Sorry. My back is in awful shape after years of play. Actually, so are my knees and wrists. But that's neither here nor there. Tell me about your family."

Quince took a drink and wadded up his trash. He stuffed it in the bag before moving to the floor with Jathan. He stretched out on his side and held his head up with hand and his elbow on the floor. Quince gave Jathan his entire focus. "I don't really talk to my family anymore. When I went to work for

Tip, my dad threw around a lot of F slurs. He made all sorts of shitty remarks about how I needed to watch my back or I might get jumped on like in that movie about two cowboys." Quince mimicked a voice he supposed was Quince's dad. "I just got fed up. Tip is like a brother to me, and he's been nothing but good to me. He's definitely done more for me than my dad ever did. I just stopped calling one day, and it really highlighted that they never called me. We never spoke again."

"Damn." Jathan didn't want him to get depressed. He flashed Quince a bright smile. "Is Quince short for Quincey or is it just Quince?"

"Just Quince. My mom wanted to name me Quincey. Dad said that was a sissy's name. His words. Not mine. So they compromised and named me Quince. What about you? I've never met another Jathan."

Jathan wasn't surprised. "My mom's name is Jan and my dad's name is Nathan, so Jathan. Apparently, that's how people always referred to them, so they thought it would be a cute name for their son." Jathan laughed. "Then they got divorced before I was a year old."

"And he's no longer in your life?"

Jathan shrugged at the question. "I went to his house every other weekend until I was fourteen and I begged to stop. Even when it was his weekend, my mom still had to come get me and take me to games and practices. He didn't have time for me. He had his new wife's two kids to worry about. I loathed going to their house. Anything that was mine at that house, they would just take and claim as theirs. Dad would just act like it was true—like he had bought whatever it was for them. I stayed enraged. So—like I said—when I turned fourteen, I begged

Mom to not make me go anymore, because it really was all her. She was the only one trying to get my dad to love me. I remember she cried for my loss, but she called him and made a deal. No more child support and I could walk away from him. When I look back on that now, I hate that I did that to her. I could've sucked it up for four more years. She was a single mom. I know she needed that child support money, but she loved me more. I got picked up at eighteen, and I promise you she's never wanted for a thing since. She's pretty fantastic. I think you'll like her."

Quince smiled. Jathan wanted to sigh at its sexiness. "I don't doubt it, but will she like me is the question?"

"Why wouldn't she?"

"I'm thirteen years older than you, for one thing."

A laugh burst from Jathan. "Do you intend to lead with that?"

Quince's eyes swam with humor. "Nah. I think it's pretty obvious when you take one look at me."

Jathan's gaze moved over Quince's face. Now that he knew Quince liked him beyond friendship, he had zero qualms about flirting. "I think you're sexy as fuck."

Heat creeped into Quince's expression. Jathan held his breath. He really hoped Quince planned to kiss him. "There's so much I want to do right now, but I'm frozen."

Jathan got it. He couldn't imagine waking up tomorrow and finding himself attracted to a woman. He thought women were beautiful, but he had never felt a sexual attraction toward one. Hearing about Quince's dad made everything clear. He had been raised in a small-minded, sexually repressed environment. Quince hadn't stood much chance of finding himself.

Jathan moved to his knees. "Don't worry. I've got this. Close your eyes."

Quince immediately closed his eyes.

Jathan gently pushed, urging Quince onto his back. "Don't look. Just feel until you know what to do." Jathan straddled Quince. He looked sexy as hell between Jathan's thighs. As much as Jathan wanted to say that, he needed to cast a spell to find Quince's breaking point.

He found the hem of Quince's t-shirt and pushed. Jathan bared two inches of skin. His fingers slipped beneath the material. He slowly moved higher, taking Quince's shirt with him.

Quince's lips parted. His entire torso moved with each breath. He breathed hard—like a nervous man anticipating pleasure. Damn.

He was gorgeous. Jathan had never wanted to kiss someone so badly. He didn't know how Quince would react yet, so he kept doing his best to steal Quince's shirt. Quince lifted slightly, letting him have the clothing he wanted so badly. Jathan's hands slid beneath Quince's armpits, urging his arms above his head. The game had him nearly nose to nose with Quince. He heard the way Quince fought to breathe. When he had Quince's hands trapped above his head by his shirt, Jathan bumped his lips against Quince's, giving him the chance to say no.

Quince rolled, pinning Jathan beneath him. His mouth covered Jathan's, and the world slipped away.

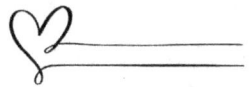

Quince had never been more aware of every inch of his body. He knew exactly each place they touched. Their kiss was the kiss he had waited his entire life to experience. Someone finally matched his hunger. There was a small part of his brain that still couldn't believe this was happening. A tiny voice screamed he kissed Jathan Dexter. Not only another guy, but a famous one. He didn't know what the hell he was doing, but his body obviously did. Quince wanted him bad.

"If you get uncomfortable at any point, you can stop."

Jathan made the claim as Quince changed angles. He was almost incredulous.

Everything inside him soared in a way he never had. He was on fire. His soul blazed. It was like he spent his entire life starved and finally found his feast. He was almost scared of how he felt.

Quince pushed at Jathan's shirt. He wanted to be skin to skin. Jathan flinched from his touch when he pushed past his ribs. Quince immediately sat back on his heels. He slowly lifted Jathan's shirt and inspected his side. It was solid black with a nasty yellow tint in several places.

"Holy shit, Jathan. What happened?"

A wry smile touched his lips. "I don't think people realize exactly how hard we're getting elbowed out there. They are actively trying to take you out of the game. I've been taking hits all season. It'll heal when I get a break."

Quince couldn't believe his ears. He kept taking hits on top of this? Jathan was tough as hell. "Are your ribs cracked? You could puncture a lung."

Jathan rolled upward, proving how strong and in shape he was with that core move. He pulled his shirt up and over his head before tossing it aside. Then he licked Quince's collarbone, obviously trying to distract him. It was working, but still.

"I'm serious, Jathan. Have they x-rayed your ribs?"

Jathan settled back down on the floor with a tired-sounding sigh. "Do you want me to sit out because I hurt a little? Do you have any idea how many people never get here? I can hurt when it's over. One of these days, I'll never get to step foot on that court again. I'll be damned if that day comes a moment before it has to. This is my dream."

Quince heard the passion in Jathan's voice. Guilt set in. "You're right. I'm sorry. What would I know about it?" He had never reached for anything he really wanted in life. Quince didn't know what it took.

Jathan's hands slid up Quince's thighs. "Don't sound like that over caring about me. That matters to me too."

Reality struck Quince. He currently straddled Jathan's body. He was in a position people would literally kill to be in. Quince had reached for this. He would be damned if he stopped now. "You should show me your bedroom."

"Help me off this floor."

Quince pushed to his feet and did his best to ease Jathan upright. Maybe he had no right to tell Jathan to care about his injuries first, but he could care. He could baby Jathan. Someone needed to. Jathan held on to his hand and headed down the hall. He pulled out his phone as he walked. After a few taps on his screen, the lights died behind them and a beeping countdown started for the alarm. It seemed he was there for the night. Good. He had no idea what he was doing, but he planned to do it anyway.

When they crossed the threshold into what Quince assumed was Jathan's bedroom, the lights flared to life and immediately dimmed to barely a glow. As long as he had been surrounded by money, he was still impressed by some people's luxuries. Quince didn't pay much attention to his surroundings. He was oddly fascinated by the way the muscles moved in Jathan's back. Jathan was extremely tall and skinny, but he was all tight muscle. He had the perfect athlete's body. It was more than obvious how active he was. Quince never much thought about other people's bodies.

He understood why now. Quince had been meant for Jathan. He didn't think he was gay or straight or even anything in between. Secretly, he had always just not been that interested in anyone. That had always made him feel odd, so he had just kept it to himself while pretending to be too busy and tired to date. Then he had spent one amazing night with Jathan. Suddenly, he had felt closer to Jathan than he had ever felt to anyone, and boom! Now it was like all the years of disinterest caught him. He had spent some time reading about things online, trying to make sense of all these sudden feelings. It seemed he was maybe demisexual or some shit like that. Whatever. He wanted to touch Jathan.

Jathan climbed onto a bed so tall, even he needed a step. Quince was right behind him. Jathan rolled onto his back and lured Quince close. "Where were we?"

"I remember." Quince took the kiss he wanted.

Jathan's fingertips skimmed Quince's stomach before reaching his belt. Chill bumps rose on Quince's skin. He sucked in his gut as Jathan went to work, undoing his belt before unbuttoning Quince's jeans. Quince wasn't losing his nerve, exactly, but he was scared of disappointing Jathan with his lack of knowledge.

"Tell me what to do right now."

Jathan urged Quince onto his back. "Enjoy." He kissed his way down Quince's chest, stroking him everywhere. All Quince could do was feel. He felt everything. Every brush of lips and fingertips and even the way Jathan's breath felt on his skin was mesmerizing. His pants loosened and eased down his hips. With his eyes closed and his entire being fully engaged, Quince lifted, letting Jathan have the rest of his clothes. He didn't have time to overthink. Jathan licked his cock. A ragged breath left his lips. He wanted to watch, but he knew if he looked, he'd blow. Quince wanted this too badly. When Jathan's hot mouth covered his dick, a sound escaped Quince even he hadn't expected. He knew to the bottom of his soul that he would leave this bed fully addicted. Quince had never experienced whatever it was Jathan did with his mouth. He wondered how long his sanity would hold. Then the suction disappeared, and Quince watched through hooded eyes as Jathan stood and stripped. He was breathtaking. Once nude, he grabbed some things from the nightstand, and then he was back. Jathan straddled his body and kissed him. Quince's cock wept in anticipation.

In a distant way, he knew Jathan worked to ready himself while he kept Quince distracted with his tongue. One day, he would need to pay attention to whatever Jathan did so he could learn to be a good partner. For now, he was transfixed. Hypnotized. Then a condom rolled down his length. A pant burst from him. There was no way he would last long enough for Jathan to come back for more. He was turned on to a level he had never experienced. Quince practically vibrated with lust.

"You're so sexy. You're handling this so good."

A breathless laugh escaped Quince at the praise. It seemed like he should be the one talking. "Are you joking? I'm trying my ass off not to blow right now. You'll definitely be disappointed tonight."

"Impossible." Jathan sat on Quince's dick.

Quince practically levitated. Only Jathan's weight kept him from flying away. "Holy shit! Oh, my God." The heat and squeezing.

He wouldn't make it. His brain quit functioning. Then Jathan bounced and Quince forgot how to breathe, causing him to make a sound like a dying donkey. Everything was equal parts mortifying and soul stealing. Jathan used his chest for leverage and rode Quince's dick like it was his favorite toy. Quince's eyes stung from his inability to even blink. He watched and memorized every moment with his muscles and teeth clenched. Quince had never held back an orgasm so long and hard in his life. It was more than pride stopping him from coming. It was desperation. This had to last as long as possible. Jathan might not want him again. The guy could have anyone. He had chosen Quince tonight. Tomorrow, who knew? Maybe he would realize Quince was unworthy. Quince couldn't stop a second before he had to.

Jathan tilted his chin up and visibly fought to come.

Quince stopped breathing. He watched Jathan get closer. It felt like it was him straining toward the edge. "Yes. Like that. I want it."

Jathan's chin dropped. Their gazes met. It was like he stared into the future. His future. Time stopped. Quince wanted this. He desperately desired a life where Jathan looked at him just like this every night. Jathan belonged to him. They were one.

"I want to know you're only mine."

Jathan blew, stealing everything from Quince. He cried out, gasping for air while Jathan's body tried sucking his soul out through his dick. It was an orgasm like none other. He felt a little weak and lightheaded. For a moment, he wondered if he would survive. His body jerked with pleasure. He couldn't control anything he did. The way his cock pulsed and spit was all he felt or knew. He probably looked like he was having a seizure.

Jathan's mouth covered his and reality slowly returned. Their tongues played lazily. His body cooled. Quince realized he trailed his fingers up and down Jathan's sides. He couldn't stop touching him and savoring the way the guy's body felt.

"Were you seriously asking to be exclusive or were you caught up in the moment?"

Quince nearly jumped at the sound of Jathan's voice. That was how deep under his trance he was. He had to swallow to be able to speak again. "I'm seriously asking."

Jathan's lips skimmed Quince's jaw before moving to his ear. "Good. That's what I want too."

"Thank God."

A sexy chuckle rumbled against his skin at his sigh of relief. Quince couldn't stop smiling. He might not have seen any of this coming, but he definitely couldn't be happier. His favorite team would soon head to the finals. Quince felt that in his blood. His favorite player was in his arms. Life couldn't be better.

Chapter Five

QUINCE DID NOT WANT to leave Jathan's bed, but he—stupidly—forgot to plan the day's work around him not being there. That didn't mean he couldn't be late.

He kissed Jathan's nape. As much as he hated to wake him, Quince hated not to say goodbye even more. "I'm sorry. You can go right back to sleep, but I have to get back to the ranch. I need to ensure everyone showed up today."

Jathan reached over his head and cupped the back of Quince's head, as if savoring the way Quince's mouth felt on his skin. He groaned. "Nooo."

Quince smiled against his neck. "Believe me, I wish I could stay." He swiped his hand over Jathan's bare hip. "I hate leaving." An idea struck. "Why don't you come with me? You can see Artem and I'll put you on a horse."

"Wakey, wakey. Eggs and bakey! We're going to breakfast." The light flared to life in the room. "Oh."

Jathan groaned.

Quince blinked at the sight of the woman in the doorway. She was likely six feet tall and skinny as hell.

"Mom. We've talked about this." Jathan sat up. The blankets slid down his sexy bare torso and pooled in his lap. "One of these days, you'll see something you really don't want to see."

She didn't look the least bit concerned. "Sorry, baby. In my defense, there's never anyone here."

Despite the situation, Quince smiled. As sad as it was, he loved knowing Jathan didn't have a different man here every night.

"Thanks for that." Jathan sounded a bit disgruntled, but he motioned Quince's way. "This is Quince. Quince, my mom."

"Jan," she added with a bright smile. "I'm heartened to hear he knows your name."

Quince chuckled as he stood and crossed the room to shake her hand. He was glad as hell he had waited to wake Jathan until after he dressed. "He'd better. It's nice to meet you."

A line appeared between her amber eyes. "Why do you look familiar to me?"

He shifted from foot to foot. "I don't know." Quince very much feared he actually did know, but that life needed to stay in the past.

She made a dismissive motion. "Anyhow, we're going to breakfast. So everyone get your shit together. I'm starving after days of being unable to eat."

"I was just headed to work."

"Oh. What do you do?"

Jathan looked like her. He had her blond hair and very similar facial features. "I'm foreman out at Tip Ramos' ranch. A ton of my workers have been out with the flu. I need to make sure everyone is covered for the day and pick up the slack where they can't."

Her smile grew. She looked like a nice person. "Oh. Artem's husband. Yeah. We've met. You're right. The flu has been fucking awful. I was about ready to beg for death."

"I'm glad to see you're feeling better."

"Personally, I'm glad everyone is having a nice conversation while I'm trapped here in the nude."

Jan waved her hand. "Please. I made that body, but I'll wait in the kitchen. Hurry. Momma's hungry." She focused on Quince for a second. "It really was nice meeting you."

"You too."

The moment she was out of sight, Jathan climbed from the bed while Quince enjoyed the show. He held up one finger. "Wait just one minute and I'll walk you out."

He wouldn't turn down that offer. "You got it." Quince's gaze followed Jathan to the bathroom. When he disappeared inside, he released the breath he hadn't realized he held. It was like Jathan wiped his entire brain. He couldn't even function normally.

Jathan reappeared after a minute, wearing a tank top and workout shorts. "Okay. I'm ready."

Quince held out his hand and smiled like an idiot all the way down the hall after Jathan accepted it. He felt ridiculously proud to be with him. In the garage, Jathan walked with him nearly all the way to his truck before he froze, pulling Quince to a stop. Quince turned.

Jathan's gaze was locked on something across the room. He dipped his chin. "Please tell me you did that?"

Quince turned his head and his blood froze. Red roses and a card rested against the windshield of his Hummer. "No. Maybe your mom." It was hopeful thinking on his part.

Jathan shook his head. The way his gaze stayed locked on the items made everything worse. It was as if he was almost scared. "You just met her. Does she strike you as the type to leave a gift on my car? She more of the burst in with balloons type."

Fuck. "Would you like me to check it out first?"

Jathan's gaze slid his way. "Would you? I know how I sound right now, but I'm also super freaked out. This has happened to me a few times in public, but this is different. There's no way into this garage without the proper signal from my phone or cars."

Yeah. Fuck this. This was unfortunately familiar territory for him. He wouldn't let this happen twice. No one scared Jathan. Quince stormed across the garage and grabbed the flowers and card. The card wasn't in an envelope. Quince flipped it open and read it aloud.

"You looked beautiful last night on that court. Why hasn't your mom been with you? There's no signature of any kind. Do you want to see if you recognize the handwriting?"

"No." Jathan looked pale. "Can you just take them with you, please?"

His reaction had Quince more than a little concerned. "Do you have any idea who these are from?"

Jathan shook his head. He looked truly shaken. Of course, as he had said, no one should be able to get into this garage.

That thought led to another. He set the flowers on the hood of the truck. "Go back into the house, baby." His eyes scanned the hundreds of places a person could hide. He didn't mean to scare Jathan, but it was best to be careful.

His words had the opposite effect. Jathan seemed to snap out of it. "I'm not leaving you out here unprotected."

Quince pulled open the driver's side door of his truck and grabbed the gun he kept in a hidden compartment under his seat. "I'm good, but I'd feel a lot better with you in the house."

Jathan gave him a jerky nod. "Okay." He headed inside, leaving Quince behind.

Quince automatically fell into his old self. That training fit like a second skin. He took his time and searched each vehicle and every corner. Quince didn't relax until he was positive Jathan was safe.

Jan poked her head out the door. "Are you still alive out here? Jathan won't let me call the police."

Quince's shoulders relaxed. "Yeah. Everything seems secure. As much as I hate to delay your breakfast, I think you should make a report. A paper trail matters."

Jan leaned against the doorframe and eyed him. "I remember now. You're that bodyguard. Jayda's bodyguard."

Quince moved to his truck and put his gun back in its holster. He couldn't and wouldn't talk about this. "Tell me what you want, and I'll grab you breakfast before I head to work." He didn't look her way as he moved the flowers and card to a nearby work table. "He asked me to take these with me, but the police will want to look for fingerprints or whatever."

"I know you're not leaving without saying goodbye."

Despite everything, Quince smiled at Jathan's sudden appearance. The guy just made his life better. "Of course not. I'm going to grab you two breakfast before I head out, so you can eat while you wait for the police." He held Jathan's stare, silently daring him to argue.

"Stay. We'll order food."

Quince didn't look to see if Jan was still there. He snagged Jathan's hips and hauled him in so he could kiss him. He fought a wave of disappointment as he pulled away. "As much as I hate it, I really have to get to work."

Jathan nodded. He looked incredibly sexy—like always—but there was also something else about him today. Damn. Quince didn't want to leave, but he couldn't stay. "Be careful driving home."

"I will." Quince stole another quick kiss before forcing himself to climb into his truck. He didn't look Jathan's way again. Quince was too weak. If he looked, he would stay.

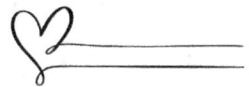

For the entire morning, Jathan felt sick to his stomach. The thought that someone had magically been inside his garage was driving him insane. After filing a police report, it had been too late for breakfast, so he had taken his mom to lunch. The meal had been... eye opening. She had gone into talking about Quince's past—like Jathan already knew everything about the man he was sleeping with. Which, fair. Jathan had just rolled with it, told his mom Quince never talked about it, and then sat back to hear all the tea. Her story explained Quince's hermit-like lifestyle. Not that Jathan had ever questioned that. He had just assumed

Quince was too busy to leave the ranch often.

Back home, he had practically run through the house, gathering things and peeking around every corner. He couldn't even bring himself to drive the Hummer. Jathan chose a car he rarely drove—his Lamborghini Huracan. For some reason, his stupid garage door didn't want to open, slowing him down. Once he got past that hurdle, he drove straight to Quince. Truthfully, that was his intention, but he also figured he could claim to be there for Artem, if necessary. No doubt Quince had already told him what had happened.

It was a two-hour drive to get to the ranch, which gave him too much time to think. Artem and he made this drive to each other all the time since Artem's move. How long would it take Quince to get tired of making it? Jathan couldn't do it all the time.

He had to focus on anything. Jathan had no idea why everything was so under his skin today. Maybe it was just nerves. This next game had everything riding on it, and damn. That was a lot of pressure. He didn't need anything else weighing on him. When the ranch came into view, Jathan forgot everything. He automatically strained to see any sign of Quince. His truck sat parked near the humongous barn, housing Tip and Artem's many horses. As he pulled into the driveway, a guy he didn't recognize stepped from the barn. It was obvious he waited to find out who Jathan was. Jathan parked behind Quince's truck and stepped out.

As he neared the barn's entrance, the guy moved his way. "Can I help you?" He was all smiles and good looks. Jathan would put him close to his age. His strawberry-blond hair whipped in the breeze and his light green eyes were all good humor. Truth be told, he looked like a player. His eyebrows rose before Jathan had time to respond. "Oh, wow. You're Jathan Dexter."

Jathan smiled. "I am." He had always been a bit uncomfortable with the fame part of his career. Jathan just wanted to play ball. "Is—"

Quince appeared behind the man. "Hey. I didn't know you were coming."

The guy between them turned slightly, giving his attention to the entire exchange.

Jathan only had eyes for Quince.

Again, before anyone let him truly talk, Artem and Tip came from the direction of the house.

Artem bounced like a kid. "Jathan! I didn't know you were coming." He rushed Jathan and hugged him.

Jathan immediately felt the weight of the world lift from his chest. From the first time they met, Artem had brought something to his life Jathan had been missing for a long time—real friendship.

"Hey." He hugged Artem back. "Yeah. Sorry for not calling."

Artem waved off his words. "You never have to, but we are—unfortunately—on our way out." He motioned the stranger's way. "Tip's brother, Sterling, is in town. We're on our way to our first and likely very disastrous dinner with Tip's mom since they started talking again."

Neither brother looked upset by Artem's words. In fact, they both smiled like they adored Artem.

Jathan nodded at Sterling. "It's nice to meet you. You're the polo player, right?"

Sterling turned twice as bright. "Yep. That's me. It's incredibly nice to meet you. How excited are you to likely be headed to the finals?"

"Ecstatic." His gaze slid toward Quince. He was impatient to touch him again. "I won't hold you up from your dinner plans. Quince can entertain me."

Artem laughed and smacked his arm. "I'll bet. Have fun. I'll hunt you down and bug you when we get back."

While wearing a huge grin he couldn't squelch, he kissed Artem's temple. "Go. Try to behave."

The three gave him a wave and said their goodbyes before heading as a unit toward a nearby SUV.

Jathan didn't watch them go. He only had eyes for Quince. "Hey. Does that offer still stand to spend the day with you?"

"Hell yeah."

Jathan's smile grew. "Maybe I can spend the night too?"

Quince motioned for Jathan to come inside the barn. Jathan followed him inside. The moment they were out of sight, Quince hauled him inside the closest stall and closed him inside. He was all over Jathan. Their mouths clashed and tongues fought. Quince squeezed his ass and Jathan was ready to do whatever he wanted.

"It's good to see you too." Jathan said between kisses.

Quince pulled away with laughter in his eyes. "Sorry."

"I'm not." Jathan snagged his shirt and pulled him back in for another kiss. "Mhmm. Damn. That's good."

"Hey, boss. You in here?"

Quince dropped his forehead to Jathan's shoulder. "Yeah. What's up?" He called the words sounding way more normal than Jathan felt.

A brown-haired guy Jathan had seen around several times poked his head over the stall door. "Oh, hey, Jathan."

Jathan smiled. "Hey, Buck."

Buck focused on Quince. "We're headed over to move the herd to the south field. The fencing is done."

"Sounds good."

Buck slapped the door twice. "See you two later."

"Always good to see you, Buck." Jathan covered his eyes.

Quince's sexy laugh had him dropping his hand. He didn't look uncomfortable with anyone knowing about them. In fact, his hands slid back down Jathan's back to hold his ass. "How was the rest of your day with your mom?"

Jathan was glad to feel normal for once. In Quince's arms, he felt oddly safe and like they created their own bubble. "I mean, after the police left, it was pretty typical. We ended up going to lunch. She teased me about not telling her about you. I didn't want to tell her last night was our first night together. You know, since she's my mom and all. Not that she knows anything about boundaries."

"I got that vibe from her."

Jathan laughed. He was just so damn happy, and Quince looked happy too. Jathan wanted time to freeze so he could hang on to the moment forever.

Quince took a step back and eyed Jathan. "Hmm... let's see. Tank top. Baseball cap.

What looks to be old jeans. You look like a man ready to work on the farm."

Jathan shrugged. "I figured if I planned to interrupt your day, then I should be useful."

Quince grabbed his hand. "Come on." He led Jathan to the back of the barn and nodded toward a ladder. "You can be useful up there."

With a shrug. Jathan climbed the ladder. A plus of being abnormally tall, it didn't take him long. It was a hayloft, which made sense. Up high was the best way to store hay.

Quince climbed the ladder behind him. "Hopefully, you're not allergic."

"Nope."

Quince smiled. "Good." He took Jathan down on the nearest pile.

A bark of laughter burst from him as he landed. Quince used his strength to break the fall, but it still had been a shock. Any time he fell, it was a long way down. Unfortunately, he tripped more often than normal people, so he would know. Quince's huge body straddled him. He stole a deep kiss. Jathan loved knowing Quince had gotten over the hurdle in his mind that had held him back.

Quince swiped his lips across Jathan's again. "Sorry. When I saw you standing in the driveway, it made me realize something. I miss you when you're not around."

"Why are you apologizing for that?"

He rolled to the side but kept one leg draped over Jathan. "I don't know. Maybe you would've thought I was being clingy. I might've scared you away."

"Dude, *I'm* clingy. If anyone should be frightened, it's you. I'll drive you crazy. You'll wonder why you ever let me have your number. Just ask Artem. I'll bet, by the end of the first night we met, he almost blocked me. He definitely already knew everything about me, down to the color of my toothbrush, because I didn't shut up all night."

Quince's smile made the confession worthwhile. "It's blue. I saw it this morning."

"What color is yours?" He loved this conversation.

"It's black."

"I can see that about you."

Jathan never tired of listening to Quince laugh.

"Did you pack a bag?"

Of course. Jathan hadn't taken any chances he might not get to stay. "Yes."

"Did you check it for AirTags?"

Damn. That took a turn. "I don't actually know how to do that, but my phone didn't alert me of any. You know how it'll sometimes tell you if you have an AirTag when you start the car."

"That's a good sign. If you let me see your phone, I can show you how to check to be certain. Just so you'll have peace of mind."

He wiggled the device from his pocket. Jathan nearly huffed when Quince didn't move his leg to give him any room to get the phone he wanted to see. Luckily, he managed it before getting aggravated. He handed it over. "I'd really have peace of mind if I knew how they got into my garage. That's bugging me more than anything."

"I'll ride home with you tomorrow and look into it," Quince said absently as he tapped around on Jathan's phone. "Okay. Look. Click on find my phone." Jathan dutifully tapped the option.

Quince kissed his ear. "Now scroll down and look for AirTags."

Jathan only had one hand with the way Quince currently seduced him. It was a good thing Quince held the phone. He tapped the AirTags option. "Okay." Even he heard how breathless he sounded as Quince kissed the spot beneath his ear.

"Scroll all the way to the bottom and it should show you any unknown tags it's picking up nearby. If you're sitting in your car, and you don't have a tag on you that's yours, then you know someone has tagged your car." Quince gave the speech while kissing Jathan's neck.

"It's a good thing I'm great at multitasking. Otherwise, I wouldn't have heard a word of that with you teasing me."

"I'm not teasing. You can put your phone away. I'm very serious."

God, he was amazing. Everything about him was temptation. "What do you plan to do?" Whoa. He sounded horny as fuck. Jathan didn't even try to reel it in.

"I haven't decided. Probably something that'll get us both really dirty."

"Mhmm. Damn. Weird way to propose, but okay."

Quince chuckled against his lips as he stole another kiss. As their tongues played, so much happiness grew in Jathan's chest that he thought he might explode.

Quince's hand slid down Jathan's stomach and didn't stop until he cupped Jathan's erection through his jeans. He massaged.

Jathan could barely breathe through the lust. A million dirty things ran through his head. He planned to do every one to Quince.

"Hey, boss. You in here?"

Quince pulled away and dropped his head on Jathan's chest. He pretended to cry before lifting his head again.

"Yeah. I'm up here. Just give me a second." His heated gaze slid Jathan's way. Sexual promise flashed at him. "Later."

Chill bumps rose on Jathan's skin at the promise. It was definitely a date.

Chapter Six

HONESTLY, QUINCE HAD THE best day with Jathan. Quince had still gotten everything done while also managing to get Jathan on a horse. He also copped as many feels as possible the entire time. Quince felt a little ridiculous admitting it, but he had never felt the way Jathan made him feel. He was way too old to have gone this long without whatever it was Jathan brought to his life, but here he was. Quince had all these crazy thoughts he wouldn't share in a million years because they were just that—crazy. The one thing shouting loudest in his head was that he wanted to keep Jathan. He never wanted to let the guy out of his sight again.

Jathan came out of the bathroom, toweling off his hair. "A man after my heart. A tall man's shower."

Quince laughed, but it was true. He was after Jathan's heart. "Don't forget, I'm a tall guy too. I built this place with that in mind."

Jathan dropped onto the couch beside him, giving Quince his full attention. "You built this place?"

"Yeah. When Tip first hired me, I stayed in the big house. Tip was never here, but for maybe one weekend out of the month—if that. I wasn't sure if I wanted to do this for the rest of my life. Since I'd been raised on a farm, and knew all about running one, it seemed like a good fit, but I'd gotten used to a different life since moving away from home."

"I imagine you traveled a lot, guarding such a huge star."

Fuck. Quince didn't know if Jathan had always known that or if his mom had filled him in. "Yeah. I was pretty much somewhere different every other day." Despite the topic, Quince smiled. "It was quite the culture shock at first. As much as I hate admitting it, I wasn't raised to tolerate anything or anyone different from me. Jayda took a huge chance on me, considering where I came from and who she was. Obviously, I completely failed her in the end. Just not in the way I expected."

He hated the sympathy in Jathan's eyes. Jathan rubbed his thigh. "You saw what happened to me this morning and I only play professional sports. That's nowhere near the fame she had. I can't imagine how hard it must've been to keep her safe. At the end of the day, no one is infallible or indestructible."

Jathan really was a good person. "As much as I appreciate the sentiment, there are lots of celebrities around the world. Mine is the one who ended up dead." Terrible flashbacks tried to suck him under. He didn't talk about those days for a reason. Quince swore he still heard the gunshots. Smelled the blood. He just hadn't seen the gun quickly enough. The world lost a shining star because he wasn't good enough. Hell, there was an entire documentary on it. To be fair, no one explicitly blamed him. There was an obsessed killer to focus on, after all, but Quince knew the truth. If he was just a little faster, then she would be alive today.

Quince couldn't talk about it anymore. "Anyhow, we got off topic. After about six years of working for Tip, I finally accepted

I wasn't going anywhere. Tip gave me five acres of land for my five-year work anniversary, so I decided to actually use them, and broke ground. I didn't need anything huge, so..." He motioned around, figuring the place spoke for itself. His house wasn't that big, but it was nice in his eyes. He liked it.

"I love it. It's very you."

A laugh burst from Quince. "What's that mean?"

Jathan shifted positions and straddled Quince. "It's quiet. Peaceful." Jathan swiped a sweet kiss across his lips. "Cozy."

Quince chuckled. "That last one sounded a lot like fat."

"You know better." Jathan ran his hands up Quince's chest. "Sexy."

Quince couldn't stop teasing him. "Country boy body. Hard-working but well fed."

Jathan snorted. "You're ridiculous."

Quince took advantage of Jathan's stance and squeezed his ass. "You're sexy."

"Actually. I kind of look like one of those orange cream pop flavored Twizzlers they had out for a while."

A loud snort escaped Quince before he could stop it. He couldn't stop grinning like a fool. "Where did that even come from?"

Jathan's smile looked so real—like he was every bit as happy as Quince, and it felt fucking phenomenal. "This guy who works at the security booth during the week was eating one when I came through one day and stopped at the gate. He looked at the candy and then looked at me. The stick he held just kind of drooped over for no reason. I don't know why, but we both burst out laughing. He said, 'just like you. Too tall for gravity.' Which is valid since I do fall over for no reason sometimes. Now I can't look at the candy without making the comparison."

Quince shook his head. "Being with you is the happiest I've ever been."

Jathan's expression softened. "No one has ever said that to me. I think people either see me as boring or as too much. Earlier, I wasn't joking. I don't get a hell of a lot of genuine human contact, so when I do, I overwhelm people."

A sad smile tugged at Quince's lips. "I don't know if you've noticed, but I live in the middle of nowhere with next to no contact with anyone outside of work. You're perfect to me."

Jathan's expression made the confession worthwhile. He bit his bottom lip and turned almost shy. Jathan twisted Quince's t-shirt, stretching it. "Well. That's a nice thing to say." He sounded like a teen, getting his first compliment. Jathan was such a conundrum to him. The guy was literally famous. People owned fan gear with his name on it. Stands were filled with screaming fans wearing his name on their jersey. But in a way, Quince got it. No one was real anymore. No doubt thousands of men were lined up to fuck Jathan, but Jathan wasn't like other people. He had a soft heart. Jathan wasn't the type to waste his time with fake people, looking just to say they had fucked Jathan Dexter. He wanted to be desired for being Jathan the person. Jathan was in the right place. Quince could easily and truthfully say he had literally never wanted a man more. He was after Jathan's heart. Quince had no plans to stop until he owned it.

"I really want to caveman-style throw you over my shoulder and storm into the bedroom right now. But I shouldn't have even tossed you in the hay earlier with those ribs looking the way they do."

"I could run in there, arms flailing, squealing like a girl, and pretending you're chasing me, if you'd like."

Jathan kept him laughing. But right now, he felt very serious. "Or I could kiss you here and hope you lead me to the bedroom the way you did last night."

"I like that option." Jathan covered Quince's mouth with his. Their tongues played. Quince couldn't stop trying to rock Jathan's body against him to get some sort of relief from the madness.

Jathan slipped from his lap, holding his hand.

Quince's mind was fully locked on making love to Jathan again. This time, he wanted to take his time. He wanted to explore Jathan's body in ways he had been too nervous to do last night.

The doorbell rang.

Quince nearly dropped to his knees from the disappointment. "Fuck! You've got to be kidding me. If someone hasn't lost a goddamn leg, they're about to." He held up one finger and stormed to the door. When he yanked it open, Quince acted without thinking. "What in the fuck are you doing here?"

Carey blinked. It obviously wasn't the welcome she expected. "Well, hi to you too."

Quince realized his first reaction had been the one that came from his heart. He didn't take it back. "Hi. What in the fuck do you want?"

"I—" Jathan's presence obviously caught her eye. Her light brown eyes widened. "Holy shit. Is that Jathan Dexter?"

Quince glanced behind him. He didn't know why. He knew who was there.

Jathan gave a small, uncomfortable-looking wave. "Hi."

The fact that Carey's presence unsettled Jathan in any way only pissed Quince off more. "Yeah. Carey, Jathan." He motioned between them. "Jathan, cheating ex."

Jathan gave him a slight smile. "Well, I'll just let you deal with that while I wait in bed."

Carey obviously didn't miss the comment, but it took her a second to react. Jathan was already gone. "Wait. What does he mean he'll be waiting in bed? What's going on?"

His patience was gone. Jathan was already in bed and Carey had already wasted too much of his life. "He means exactly what he said. He's waiting in my bed exactly where he should be since he's mine. In case you still don't get it, I'm also his. Don't come back." He shut the door in her face and locked it before turning out all the lights, including the porch light. Normally, Quince would never be such a dick, but he had already given her more chances than any man alive would. It was time for her to move along—the way Quince had already done. A sexy man waited for him in bed. Quince had found his place. He fully intended to embrace every moment. Jathan was everything now.

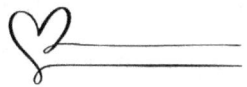

A cheating ex. Jathan wondered how long the two had been split if she was still showing up at his house. He stripped and climbed into bed, waiting the way he had said he would. But Jathan wondered now if he should have said that. It was possible Quince might react badly—like he had when he first realized he wanted Jathan.

While Quince hadn't jumped away from Jathan when Buck had shown up earlier, he also hadn't truly acknowledged Jathan when he arrived until after they had been alone and out of sight. Maybe he should put his clothes back on just in case Quince turned cold again. The last thing he wanted was to need to get dressed while trying to storm out.

He threw back the covers and sat up. Quince appeared in the doorway. Jathan had left the light on in the bathroom and the door open, so Quince wouldn't trip in the dark. The light highlighted Quince's hungry features.

"Goddamn. When you said you'd be waiting, I didn't picture this. That's a lie. I immediately pictured this, but figured it wouldn't happen."

Jathan laughed. He didn't bother covering his nudity. "I mean, apparently, I'm competing with an ex tonight."

Quince padded toward him. "You absolutely aren't. There's no comparing to this." He pushed, urging Jathan onto his back before straddling him fully dressed. "Unfortunately, a horrible thought hit on my way in here. I don't have any lube here. Like, we have plenty out and around the ranch for several reasons, but I've never really had a reason."

He was adorable. "That's okay. I have other ways I can make you happy."

"I'm already happy. In fact, before you, I couldn't figure out why I was so fucking unhappy. It was like I went with the flow, but nothing more. I never went out of my way to get into anyone's bed. If I ended up there, then whatever, but I never tried. It's like you filled me with life or something. I can't really explain it. It's like it's not about sexual orientation or attraction or anything like that. It's just this." He motioned between them. Quince was so seen and he didn't even know it.

Jathan wouldn't let him think he was the odd one out. "It sucks pretty hard when you don't know that about yourself yet—when you don't recognize you're not really sexually attracted to anyone without there being something else there. That feeling used to make me feel like more of an outsider than anything else about me and I'm pretty fucking awkward."

He took Quince's hand and used it to stroke himself from his chest downward. "I very much want you to touch me, though. You're all I think about."

Quince licked his lips. He suddenly looked nervous as hell. The steely eyes that were always filled with so much confidence looked unsure now. "I really want to do everything with you, but I'm not sure how." An adorable blush covered his face as he made the confession, but Quince kept going. "It's crazy how badly I want to taste your dick, but I don't want to fail you. You've probably had a ton of sexy men on their knees with all the experience I'll never have."

Jathan fought a snort. "Did we just meet or something?" He couldn't hide the humor in his voice. "Surely you can't really believe that about me."

Quince shrugged. "I think you're famous and people are probably lined up to do exactly what I want to do; except they actually know what the fuck they're doing."

He truly sounded upset. Jathan couldn't have that. "First things first. Even if I had a line of men around the block on their knees, I'm damn near seven feet tall. Most men would be staring at my kneecaps." A smile exploded across Quince's face. Jathan kept going. "In second place, can you imagine me in that situation? I'd just be blushing and begging people to please stand up."

Jathan ran his hands up Quince's thighs. "Lastly, I find you so fucking hot that I could probably blow just from having you breathe too hard on my dick. You're the one who makes me want to talk dirty, pull hair, and bite. I don't blush with you."

His hand moved to the bulge in Quince's pajama pants. He stroked. "You shouldn't blush with me either. Whatever you want to try with me, I'm in. I'm always silently begging for you to touch me. It's been that way since we met."

Quince leaned forward and braced his weight on his hands on either side of Jathan's head, boxing him in. He swiped his lips across Jathan's. "Talk me through it."

The muscles in his stomach cramped with need at Quince's demand. "I promise I'll love whatever you do."

Quince kissed him. It turned heated fast. Jathan was already panting when Quince began his slow descent. He dug his fingertips into Quince's sexy shoulders, trying to cling to sanity. Jathan kind of worried he might blow before Quince's mouth ever touched him. He couldn't believe Quince thought there was any chance of Jathan not enjoying anything he did. Jathan was just happy to be there. Finally, a hot tongue slid down his length.

Jathan's entire body reacted. His toes curled. "Oh, God. You're doing great."

He felt Quince's soft chuckle as he lightly sucked Jathan's crown.

Jathan didn't even care Quince laughed at him. "Yes. Like that."

Quince took more of him and saliva rolled down his length.

"Jesus. You've got this." Jathan focused on breathing as Quince worked his cock. He felt the way Quince kept trying to go farther before backing off again. The move reminded Jathan he was supposed to be helping. He swiped his fingers through Quince's dark hair. It was so fucking soft. He fought the urge to pull. "If you want to try to take more, just relax your throat. Don't think about it too much. Just—" The words died on a strangled cry as his cock hit the back of Quince's throat. Everything felt too good. He wasn't going to make it. Two more downward bobs and Jathan's entire body seized. Sounds escaped him. He didn't try to hold them back. Jathan also didn't wait to see how Quince reacted to cum filling his mouth. He sprang, flipping Quince onto his back. With only the slightest tug, he had Quince's dick out and in his mouth. He didn't bother pulling his pants down enough to do more than free his cock. Jathan sucked, giving Quince the full treatment while his brain was still half trapped in the aftermath of his orgasm. He bobbed on Quince's erection, taking him down his throat. Jathan squeezed and sucked. He licked while saliva poured down his hand when he pumped. Quince sounded like a wild animal. Jathan didn't let up even when he felt Quince's body stiffen. A shout cut through the air and hot cum coated his tongue. Jathan swallowed and tried for more. He licked away every drop.

Quince wheezed like he had run a marathon. "Holy shit. Goddamn. I can't think."

Jathan kissed a path up Quince's body. He stopped to pay homage to Quince's nipples.

Quince lightly cupped the back of his head. His body still shook slightly, making Jathan proud. "Damn, Jathan. That was... fuck."

Jathan captured his mouth, smothering the praise. That hadn't been talent, practice, or skill. Jathan just craved Quince's body in a way he never had before. It was them. They were explosive and Jathan would be goddamned if he ever willingly let go.

Chapter Seven

N<small>O</small> <small>MATTER HOW HARD</small> he tried, Quince couldn't stop bringing Jathan's hand to his mouth and kissing it while Jathan drove. The sweet smile that popped to Jathan's lips each time had Quince fascinated. That smile was for him.

Jathan slowed as he reached the gate of his community. The thick iron piece slowly rolled back. Jathan lowered his window. "Good morning, Steven."

A young-looking guard in the guard shack was all smiles as he waved. "Good morning."

The fencing finally moved enough for them to enter. Jathan rolled up his window and pulled through.

"Twizzler guy?"

A bark of laughter burst from Jathan, making Quince smile. "Yep. That's him."

Quince couldn't tear his eyes away from Jathan. That was why he didn't miss the first hint of confusion that set in.

"Okay. That's weird."

Quince looked toward the road. He was a little surprised they were already in Jathan's driveway. Quince had gotten lost staring. "What's up?"

"The garage door isn't opening again. I thought it was just a fluke when I left yesterday. The Chiron had no problems when I took Mom to lunch."

"Asking a poor man question, but what triggers it to open?"

"Each car has a sensor installed."

Quince nodded. "Is there another way?"

Jathan grabbed his phone and clicked around. "The door opened." They pulled in.

Quince opened his door. "Show me where this sensor is. I can probably figure it out."

Jathan flashed him a smile. "My Jack of all trades." He popped the hood.

They climbed from the car.

Side by side, they stood staring down at the inner workings of another extremely expensive car. Quince tried not to drool and be practical. He waited for Jathan to point out the sensor. When Jathan didn't, he looked over to find Jathan looking even more confused.

"What?"

"It's gone."

Quince's blood went cold. "Show me where it's supposed to be."

Jathan pointed to an area where there was no way it could have fallen off. He saw immediately how it would be installed to get power. It had to have been taken off the car by force.

"I think it's time for you to hire a bodyguard."

Jathan closed the hood. "I have you."

Quince fought a growl. "Seriously, Jathan. This is very likely how that person got in your garage. How long has it been since this car has been driven?"

Jathan shrugged. "I don't know. Months."

"Did the door open when you came home then?"

"I don't know. I didn't take it out. There's a guy who does that on rotation, so the cars don't just sit."

Quince massaged his forehead. Someone could have been coming in for literal months and Jathan didn't want security. He dropped his hand. Quince had a bad feeling this wasn't the first thing Jathan chose to ignore.

"Were those flowers the first?"

Jathan shifted from foot to foot, making Quince's heart sink. "Well, I mean. That's the first time anyone has ever gotten inside, but I've had gifts left elsewhere. That's pretty common."

"Have you filed reports? Made a paper trail?"

Jathan shifted from foot to foot again.

Quince threw his arms up. "Damn it, Jathan. People are nuts. Are you trying to end up hurt? Even if this wasn't happening, what about crazed fans who want to take you out of the game to ensure their team wins? You're so much bigger than you realize."

Jathan grabbed his overnight bag from the car without responding.

Quince crowded his space before he got away. "I can't be with you all the time. Why would you make me worry like this?" Quince tried to become as pitiful as possible. "Are you trying to break my heart?" He kissed Jathan's neck. "Don't do this to me."

Jathan laughed at his over-the-top ridiculous tone. "Okay. I'll think about it. I'll ask around. See if anyone has any recommendations."

At the end of the day, that was all Quince could ask. He couldn't force Jathan to hire someone. Quince hugged him tightly against his chest. His throat swelled. "I've seen this, and I can't live it twice."

Jathan melted into him. "No fair. You know I'd never hurt you."

Quince didn't give a shit if he played dirty. He had all the feels for Jathan. If anything happened to him, Quince might not survive it. Sometimes there wasn't enough therapy in the world.

He took a step back. "Now. Remind me again what all we have to do before game time."

Jathan took his hand and headed for the door. "A ton of shit, actually. With it being the deciding game, I have to get to the stadium early for interviews and all that. You'll probably be bored off your ass to..." Jathan froze inside the doorway.

Out of pure instinct, Quince yanked Jathan out of the doorway and shoved him behind him. His entire kitchen counter was filled with gifts and flowers.

Jathan kissed his nape and tugged him backward against his chest. "It's okay. I was just caught off guard after yesterday. I forgot my management team was scheduled to come by. It always looks this way after they've vetted and approved my fan mail."

"Holy hell." Quince stepped inside. He was completely speechless. Once he moved far enough into the room, he realized there were boxes of shit piled on the floor on the other side of the kitchen island.

"Surely, Jayda had it worse."

Quince shook his head as he moved to eye all the flowers and cards. "I never saw her deal with her mail. She hired a company to answer everything. I doubt she saw a single thing anyone sent."

"That's kind of shitty. Then again, I can't imagine how much stuff she must've received. I was a kid when she died, so I don't know much about her."

Quince groaned. "I've never felt so old."

Jathan flashed him an evil grin as he moved to the counter and began opening cards on the flowers. "People spend their time and money on this stuff. The least I can do is take a look. I let management send people the thank-you notes and whatnot, though. I don't have that kind of time."

He fascinated the fuck out of Quince. It was no wonder someone hardcore stalked him. He was too nice for his own good. Still, Quince couldn't resist this peek inside a famous athlete's life. Jayda's life had been totally different. She had been on twenty/four-seven. A camera had always been in her face. Jathan's was a different shade of fame. "What do you do with all of this?"

Jathan shrugged. "I have a gift room upstairs. When it gets out of control, someone on my management team arranges to have everything donated to charity."

"You really have like an entire management team, don't you?"

Jathan met his stare, looking confused by the question. "Doesn't Tip?"

Quince shrugged. "I run his ranch and keep his land safe. That's all he hired me to do. I don't get into his business."

Jathan went back to looking at his letters. "Oh. That's cute." He held a crayon drawing. It was obviously supposed to be Jathan.

A smile snapped to Quince's lips. "Adorable." A thought occurred to him when he noticed—oddly—one gift was a toaster.

It had the team logo on it, but still. "Hey. Do people do that shit where they send you wedding invitations just to see if you'll send a gift?"

Jathan laughed. "Yeah. I send them a letter of apology for missing their wedding, along with a signed basketball card."

Quince shook his head. "All this and you still don't realize you need security."

Jathan made a dismissive gesture. "You've been out with me. People don't usually bother me. If they do, it's asking for a selfie, and they're always super nice about it. I think most people don't want to look like a psycho fan." A bright smile lit his face. "I saw Lady Gaga one time at a party. Never in my life have I wanted to make a fool of myself like I did that night. I didn't bother her, though. She's allowed to have some peace."

Quince shook his head. He couldn't imagine what it looked like inside Jathan's head. The guy really was all sunshine, rainbows, and kindness.

"I've never felt so lucky to know someone in all my life, and that has nothing to do with your job. You're easily the greatest person I've ever met."

Jathan looked confused but moved. He closed the gap between them. Jathan crowded his space and wrapped his arms around Quince's neck. His lips skimmed Quince's. "That sounds like some shit a guy trying to get in my pants would say."

A growl escaped Quince. He slapped Jathan's ass. "Don't toy with me."

With a laugh, Jathan took a step back. "We have an hour before we have to leave. Do you want to go through all this stuff with me?

If you see anything you want, you can have it."

Quince didn't hesitate. "Sounds fun." It genuinely did. The nosey side of him had to know what sort of things people sent their favorite basketball player. The rest of Quince just wanted to be in Jathan's company. It didn't matter what they did. They were together. He felt like he had waited his entire life for this.

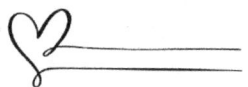

If this motherfucker didn't stop checking Jathan in the ribs, Jathan was about to get tossed from this game. His rage level was through the roof. It was only matched by his pain. Goddamn. Sometimes a season could be long as hell. Then the clouds parted. Angels sang. Jathan smirked. He saw his chance. In a quick move, he shifted just enough to goad the guy into another sharp elbow to the ribs. This time, Jathan had seen the ref's eyes on them.

The whistle blew. "That's two."

Jathan shot the guy a shit-eating grin. Free throws were like child's play to him. All net. Zero interferences. Swoosh. Both shots made.

"Yeah. Keep that shit up, motherfucker. I can make those all night."

Just another game. That was all Jathan kept telling himself until that final buzzer sounded. Then, an explosion of sound loud enough to nearly deafen him blasted through the air. Several violent hugs, lifting him from his feet, might have had him crying out in pain if not for the adrenaline. Jathan's gaze automatically swept toward the place where his mom and Quince should be and he was there, carried straight to Jathan with the flood of the crowd on to the floor. His huge smile made everything perfect. Still, he let Jathan's mom launch herself at him first. She had never cared how sweaty he was.

"Oh my, God! You did it!" The screeching mixed with everyone else's. He felt like the room was spinning with so much happening around him. People were being ushered off the court. Media was everywhere. He was overwhelmed as hell until Quince's arms wrapped around him. His mind went quiet. All he heard was Quince's voice against his ear.

"I'm so proud of you. If you don't get them ribs X-rayed, I'm going to put you over my knee."

A laugh burst from Jathan.

Quince's mouth covered his, and Jathan left everything behind. This really was the one for him. Then he was in a group hug with his mom and Quince—like life was just happening to him. He felt outside of himself. His heart finally began to slow, bit by bit. He took the first full breath he recalled taking in a while. Things came clearer into focus. He felt in control of his mind again.

Jathan's coach slapped his shoulder. "Time to move."

Jathan nodded. He focused on his mom and Quince. "I have to go. I'll meet you at the car."

They both nodded and took turns kissing him before he jogged away. Things were just as nuts inside the locker room. The room only quieted long enough for their coach's speech and then was right back to everyone talking over each other. Jathan rushed through his shower and grabbed his things. He was stopped four times for various interviews outside the locker room before finally making it to the parking garage. His mom sat in the passenger seat of his Hummer. Quince was in the back. They were both oddly stoic when Jathan opened the door.

"Hey. Is everything okay? It's awful quiet in here." He was still riding a high. Jathan wanted the people in his corner to be the same. His phone rang before anyone responded. It was Artem. "Hang on." He pressed the device to his ear. "Hello?"

A squeal cut through the line so loud, he had to pull the phone away for a second. "Oh, my God! I'm so proud of you. Tip is already talking to his people to get tickets for all the finals games as soon as they're offered. No matter what it takes, we'll be there. You must be so ecstatic."

"I really am."

"And, oh my goodness, every channel has showed that kiss with Quince. You two look so adorable and happy. I'm just over the moon for you right now."

"Thank you. It makes everything that much better to have you here in spirit."

His mom made a slight motion with a card that caught his attention. Artem fell into a rambling monologue. His mom's dark expression made his heart rate kick up. He reached for the card while Artem rambled. It had bright red hearts and kisses all over the front. He opened it and read.

It was so nice watching you walk in tonight. You look beautiful. I'm also glad to see your mom is feeling better and that you've hired security. Not that I think you've made a good choice. One person has already gotten killed on that guy's watch. Nonetheless, you need someone. You're too easy to get to. Good luck tonight. I can't wait to watch you win.

Jathan's blood ran cold as he read the card.

"Are you still there?"

Artem's question pulled Jathan from his silent panic. "Yeah. Sorry. There's a lot going on, splitting my attention, but I'm still here."

"Damn. I'm sorry. I got carried away. Obviously, you're crazy busy. You can call me as soon as things calm down. I just wanted you to know I love you and I'm so, so proud of you."

"Thank you. I love you too. I'll call you in the morning."

"Okay. Tell your mom and Quince I said hi, and have fun."

"I will. Bye."

"Bye, sweetie."

Jathan hit end and stared at nothing.

"I called an old buddy of mine who runs a security service. He's sending a guy over later. You can interview him if you want, but the service runs on a rotation of people who've all been carefully vetted. You can choose to stick with them or not. I'm covering it until you decide. You can't wait any longer."

Jathan nodded at Quince's speech. He got it. Whoever this was had walked into a secured area and watched him enter the building, left a card in his car, and probably watched him now. Jathan swallowed. He wouldn't let this change who he was. Jathan passed the card to Quince. "I'll let you decide what to do with that, but I'm not letting this ruin our night. Okay?" His gaze moved between Quince and his mom. "I worked too hard to get here to let a nameless, faceless person take it away."

They both nodded.

"Let's keep our plans."

Jathan gave a sharp nod at his mom's words and started the car. As he pulled from the lot, the air still felt heavy. It took a few minutes before his mom spoke, cutting through the tension. She chatted happily. He smiled and nodded, doing his best to breathe. Quince's phone rang and chirped a few times. He openly ignored it. That had Jathan's curiosity rising and lifted the final bits of ugliness from his brain. When they made it to the exclusive restaurant his mom chose so they could celebrate, Jathan was ready to burst. Quince kept silencing his phone, even as he opened Jathan's door and blatantly transformed into his bodyguard. His phone still vibrated. Jathan felt it against his side.

Quince looked in every direction, visibly searching for any signs of danger.

Jathan couldn't take it. "Seriously, who in the fuck is blowing up your phone? I just won the playoffs, and only one person has called me." He tried infusing as much humor as possible in his tone, but his nerves were bad tonight. Any mystery at all was too much.

"Sorry. I'll turn it off. I didn't want to miss any calls or texts from the security service, but my dad won't stop calling."

That brought Jathan's mind to a halt. Unfortunately, he had to wait until they were seated before he could respond. "Why aren't you answering?" He kept his voice low, keeping their conversation between them while his mom ordered champagne.

"I made that mistake while walking out of the stadium. His first words were, 'I told you being an f slur was contagious.' So I hung up on him and now he won't stop calling. Nothing in twelve years. Now, this." Quince sounded every bit as hurt as he should. His dad was obviously a piece of shit.

"Text your guy my number and then turn off your phone. You don't deserve this. I'll pay to have your number changed tomorrow and don't worry about covering security. I've got it. You don't have to worry that I'll refuse their help."

A sweet smile touched Quince's lips. "You don't have to do—"

"I know you don't drink, baby, but I still ordered champagne. If you'd like something else to toast with, just let me know."

Jathan swiped his hand up Quince's thigh beneath the table. "Yeah. I'll figure it out, since I'm driving and all."

Quince cut in. "I'll drive. You celebrate. Not only do you deserve a glass of champagne, you probably need it because I've seen those ribs that asshat kept elbowing."

Jathan's shoulders fell the second his mom's gaze sharpened. "What about your ribs?"

"It's fine. They're just a little bruised from the season. You know how dirty these guys play anytime they can get away with it." He squeezed Quince's knee, silently daring him to keep talking.

Unfortunately, his mom's momma bear side appeared. "Let me see."

"Mom, we're in the middle of a nice restaurant. I'm okay. Pretty soon, I'll have six long months of healing time."

She didn't look appeased, but she dropped it. His phone buzzed as the champagne arrived, along with glasses of ice water. He checked the face.

Unknown number: *this is Steel from Steel Security. Quince gave me your number. I have a guy meeting you at eleven at the address provided. His name is German. I'm sending you his picture and info so you'll know him when you see him.*

Jathan: *Thank you. Let me know how billing works, and I'll take care of it.*

Jathan saved the number to his contacts.

Steel: *Quince has already covered a month of service. If you decide to stick with our company, I'll be glad to go over the details with you. It's nice to meet you and I'm sorry you're going through this. Don't worry. I only employ the best. We won't let anything happen to you.*

Jathan: *I appreciate it.*

A wave of relief washed over Jathan.

Steel: *You're more than welcome and congrats on tonight's win. Huge fan.*

A smile exploded across Jathan's face. He put his phone away and picked up his glass. Jathan shouldn't have been so stubborn about this. He felt better already. Quince kissed his temple while his mom made a toast. Warmth spread through chest. Everything would be okay. He didn't need to worry.

Chapter Eight

QUINCE WATCHED JATHAN GO through every emotion possible throughout the night. He thought maybe he should feel something about hearing from his dad after twelve long years. Maybe he would if the man had chosen anything else at all to say. Of course, he hadn't, though. That was his old man—a bastard through and through. He hadn't thought much about his family in a long time. Quince didn't like looking back on his childhood. His dad had been low key physically abusive and high key mentally abusive. Quince had run for his life at eighteen. Steel was the only reason he had gotten free. They had gone to high school together and had been equally motivated to get the fuck out of their small town. Unlike Quince, Steel had come from money—as far as small-town money went. His dad was the local steel mill owner who employed everyone within forty miles... so about two hundred people. Steel had been his best friend and had access to all the high-dollar latest technology. His dad had put Steel to work at thirteen. He paid the kid good but worked him half to death. Turned out, whatever that home life was like, it was enough to beef Steel up to six-two and two fifty-five of pure muscle, line his pockets with a huge nest egg, and pay for all the tech skills needed to walk away at nineteen. Since Quince had been right at his side nearly all their lives, he had walked away right next to him. Quince had been Steel's very first employee. Together, they had landed some huge fucking contracts. Unfortunately, a decade later, everyone knew how that story ended: with a client dead and Quince done with playing hero.

Now here he was again, watching someone's back while they walked their mom to the door. The thing was, back in the day, Quince had really loved this job. He had honestly thought he was good at it, and he had felt a sense of purpose. It was dangerous, but important. There were real people trapped behind the fame. Good people like Jathan. He didn't deserve to live in fear, all because he loved basketball and was good at it. But some batshit insane person out there probably thought Jathan made eye contact with him once or sent subliminal messages through his TV screen. Who knew what went on in people's heads? No matter how it happened, obsessed people did desperate things, and Quince felt more than his old sense of duty. This was personal. Jathan was his. He couldn't let anyone harm him.

Quince had watched Jathan stop and take more selfies and sign more autographs than usual tonight. The entire time, his heart had been in his throat, wondering if every face he saw was the person who had their sights set on Jathan. The moment they were alone and locked inside Jathan's Hummer, Quince was across the seat and on him. His heart needed soothing.

Sometimes, it struck him at the most random moments how much he had changed and how quickly it had happened. All it had taken was the right person and Quince was ready to do everything he had never done and feel all the things he had never felt. He was falling hard as hell for Jathan.

Jathan ran his fingers through Quince's hair. "We should definitely get back to my place."

Quince had to force himself to pull away. "Yeah. I need to see how bad those ribs look now."

A loud snort came from Jathan's side of the car. "You're really not going to let this go, are you?"

A huge grin split Quince's face as he pulled away from Jan's house. "I'm really not going to let this go. Someone has to look out for you since you won't."

"Oh, dang. It's almost eleven. Steel said that German guy will be at my place then. I'd hope to drag you to bed, but I guess not."

"He won't care if we go straight to bed. It's not your job to entertain him. In fact, if we're in bed, then he's free to roam the property or watch TV. Whatever. Maybe he can stake out the garage and catch this person."

"That is the best-case scenario, really. One night of security and problem solved."

Quince shot him an annoyed look. Jathan really thought he could just catch this guy and go back to life as usual.

Jathan burst out laughing. "Your face. Jesus. I can practically hear you cursing at me in your head. Don't worry. I don't intend to drop security whenever this person is caught. It would just be nice to be out from underneath this worry. I'm not used to feeling threatened."

That was because he was so damn nice, he wouldn't recognize a threat if it bit him. Quince wouldn't be surprised if this wasn't the guy's first stalker, but they gave up from frustration after Jathan was too blind to notice he was being stalked.

Jathan ran his hand down Quince's arm. "I know I don't show it, but I appreciate you worrying about me. That's just a new feeling for me. I'm used to everything being on me."

Quince tossed a glance Jathan's way. He wished he was better with words. "Yeah, well. I kind of like you." Their fingers linked. Quince's chest swelled with pride and something else. "Maybe I more than like you. I guess it's kind of dumb." He was glad to be driving. He didn't have to look at Jathan. "You've been coming around the ranch for over a year now, teasing me. Making me feel things. I think that's made me feel closer to you than I should this early in things." He would scare Jathan if he kept going. Quince needed to stop. "Anyhow, I told you I was clingy, and you'll maybe run screaming from this relationship."

"No. I get what you're saying. It's like we danced around each other or something, just enough to feel like we were already dating. Now I sound crazy."

Actually, that was the perfect description. "You sound like you're better at describing what I was trying to say. We don't feel new. I feel like you've been mine, and I just didn't have the nerve to admit it."

"Yeah." The softly spoken word sounded like a caress. "You feel a lot like my forever person."

Quince looked his way as they waited for the gate to open at Jathan's subdivision. Their gazes met and held. "Yeah. Same."

They shared a smile before Quince went back to driving. A motorcycle sat at the curb in front of Jathan's house and a man inspected the outside of the garage.

Before Quince had time to go on full alert, Jathan piped up. "Oh. That looks like the guy Steel sent me a picture of earlier: German."

Quince was beyond relieved he was already there. He was more than ready to take Jathan to bed and hold him. He slowed as he pulled into the driveway and rolled down the window as he neared German.

German approached the car. "Hey. Sorry I'm a little early. Steel was telling me about how it was your garage this guy keeps getting in, so I wanted to check it out. Oh, I'm German." He was the typical guard: big, mean-looking, yet personable.

Jathan leaned toward the open window. "Hey, German. It's nice to meet you. You can pull your bike into the garage, if you'd like. There's plenty of room."

He nodded. "Sounds good. I'll meet you in there in a second and we'll quickly go over a few things. I'm sure you're ready for bed."

"Definitely."

Quince didn't miss the undertone.

He smirked without thinking.

German looked his way and walked away with laughter dancing in his eyes. Yeah. He would be a good fit for Jathan.

Jathan dug out his phone and clicked around while they slowly pulled into the garage. "I'm just setting this up so the door doesn't close behind us and German can pull in."

That reminded him of something he had meant to ask earlier. "You said there's a guy who comes by to take your cars out on rotation, and someone was here earlier to drop off your mail. How many people have access to your home?"

Jathan made a noise—like he thought it over—as he slipped from the Hummer. "Let me see."

Quince followed behind him.

Jathan made it three steps and froze. A guy dressed in all black who looked no more than twenty stepped into the open.

His nose and eyes were red, as if he had been crying. "What are you doing with him? You're supposed to be mine."

Quince moved to put himself bodily between the two. He made it two steps before the guy had a gun pointed at him. It didn't shake. He fully intended to kill someone.

"You stay where you are. This is all your fault. I know you seduced him. Jathan would never hurt me otherwise."

"Look at me, Isaac."

The kid's gaze snapped to Jathan. It was obvious Jathan knew him. There was so much love in Isaac's expression when he looked at Jathan that it was terrifying. There was no way everyone in this room would walk away from this.

"Talk to me, Isaac. Tell me what's going on."

It was obvious Jathan kept saying Isaac's name to emphasize he knew him and to keep Isaac's focus. "I saw him kiss you. Everyone did. Why would you let him do that?" The more he spoke, the higher his voice went. Jathan wouldn't be talking him down from this. "I've been really good to you. I know you've gotten my gifts. What has he given you?" He took a step closer, shaking the gun at Jathan.

Quince eased closer.

"Drop the gun!"

At German's appearance, Quince saw the moment Isaac lost hope. Quince leapt, throwing himself in front of Jathan.

"I'm sorry."

In a distant sort of way, he heard the gun fire. He just couldn't understand why he couldn't draw a single breath. German looked like an avenging angel appearing from nowhere and taking Isaac to the floor. Oddly, though, they stared at each other from the floor—like time froze for both of them. The pain in Isaac's expression burned its way into Quince's brain. He had the strangest thought. If he lost Jathan, he imagined he would look just like that. It seemed that would be the last thing he ever saw. He tasted the blood choking him now. That was a shame.

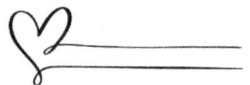

Jathan stared at the wall. It was like his brain had shut down and he couldn't function. His mom came with a bag packed for him. All Jathan could do was sit there with Quince's blood covering him. People spoke to him. He didn't hear them or remember anything they said. Eventually, Artem shoved him into the hospital room bathroom and forcibly showered the blood from him. It wasn't until he was clean and a stranger burst into the room that Jathan came to life.

The elderly man eyed the bed and heavy blankets that hid Quince from sight. His gaze moved to the machines currently keeping Quince alive. Jathan's new security team surrounded the guy, looking unsure of what to do, which was fair. The guy looked like he would break if they grabbed him.

"I knew this would happen. His mother and I tried to tell him where this lifestyle would lead him."

"Get out." Jathan didn't have it in him to listen to this bullshit. Quince wouldn't want him here.

Quince's dad looked taken aback by the hatred and rage in Jathan's voice. That didn't stop him, though. "This is my son. I'll be the one who decides what happens from here."

Jathan couldn't do this. His gaze moved to German.

German gave him a nod and stood.

Jathan didn't even watch German toss him from the room. His gaze returned to the wall. His entire being focused on the sound of the machine breathing for Quince. This was his fault. If he had taken things more seriously sooner, then maybe things wouldn't have gotten this far. Jathan simply existed while life happened around him. His mom came and went. Tip made sure everyone understood Quince had given Tip power of attorney years ago. No one would make decisions except him. As days passed, life slowly returned to him. He didn't have a choice. Jathan played his finals and somehow won in a blowout of four straight games. He had no clue how it happened. His brain never left Quince's side. Even the jaw-dropping drama surrounding one of the team's ball boys stalking Jathan to the point of attempted murder didn't shake Jathan from his nightmare.

Quince hit milestones. Doctors claimed he was getting better. Still, he didn't wake up. There was a very real possibility he never would. If he did, there was no telling what damage the massive blood loss had caused. There was also no way of knowing how much the damage to his lungs would affect the quality of his life. He still couldn't believe a single bullet had done so much damage. Apparently, those things bounced around. Quince's heart had been grazed before the bullet ricocheted to tear through his lung. It hadn't stopped until the most damage possible had been done. Jathan didn't understand the science behind that. It didn't matter, since the outcome was the same. Jathan's heart had been ripped from his chest, and he couldn't handle the pain.

The door opened, and Sterling stuck his head in. "Is it okay if I come in?"

Jathan nodded.

Sterling slipped into the room and found a chair. "Tip had to work today. I volunteered to come sit with you. It seems you're not eating or anything unless someone feeds you like they would a toddler."

Jathan managed a sad smile, but he didn't feel like chatting. Tip's little brother seemed like the chipper type. Jathan supposed people normally saw him the same way. How exhausting. No wonder he didn't have many friends.

"Quince put me on my first horse."

Jathan focused on Sterling. His light green eyes stayed locked on Quince as he spoke. "I practically lived out in that barn as a kid."

Sometimes Jathan forgot Quince was older than him. He had no clue how old Sterling was, but he got the impression the guy was at least slightly younger than him. "I thought you lived with your mom." Even Jathan had to admit he sounded like shit. His voice sounded like it hadn't been used in decades.

Sterling focused on him. He truly looked young. "I did. The property Tip bought for her is across the street and up the road a hair. Not too far to walk. I hated it at home, so I followed Quince everywhere and drove him crazy."

Jathan smiled at the image Sterling painted. "I'm sure he wasn't bothered. He likes to grumble, but he's a softie."

Sterling smiled. "Maybe, but I was a pretty annoying kid. I always had a million questions, but I was terrified of horses. One day, he snatched me from the ground and tossed me onto one. I just froze." A chuckle fell from Sterling's lips. "He took the horse's lead and walked in a circle, waiting me out."

"And the rest was history? Now you're a famous polo player."

A bark of laughter burst from Sterling. "No, and hardly. I'm mediocre at best. I told him I was telling Mom and stormed away."

"What did your mom say?"

Sterling's smile turned sad. "It was an empty threat. She didn't know I existed. But I slipped into the barn when I thought Quince had gone home and pet the horse I had ridden. I'd never fallen in love so quickly with an animal and I've owned a ton." He nodded Quince's way. "Unfortunately,

Quince had not gone home for the night, and he was furious. I honestly could have gotten hurt. I didn't know anything about horses since I had always been too scared to mess with them. They're not all evenly tempered. Tip owned a few that could've easily stomped me to death. He made me muck out stalls for a week afterward. Not that he had any real authority over me, but I knew if I wanted to keep coming back, I'd take my punishment. Since no one else ever spoke to me, I didn't want to lose that connection."

Sterling looked Quince's way. "It's tough to see him like this. He's always seemed invincible to me." He met Jathan's stare again. "But I know this won't beat him. He's too ornery. Any day now, he'll wake up pissed off that he missed you win that championship."

"It doesn't mean anything if I lose him." Jathan didn't care if he sounded dramatic. No one understood. Before Quince, no one had given him every second of their time the way Quince had. He had Artem, but Artem had Tip and his family. Jathan saw his mom once a week, but he had desperately needed something more when he had dragged Quince into his life kicking and screaming. Jathan's mood lifted a hair at the thought. He had really thrown a basketball at full speed at the man's back and caveman-style claimed him as his. This was killing him.

Sterling stood. "Do you want something to eat? You should probably have something. All of this is pointless if you don't look after yourself too."

"The kid's right, Jathan. You need to eat."

Jathan startled at the sound of German's voice from the corner. The guy was so quiet, he was nearly invisible, especially in Jathan's barely aware state.

A huge grin split Sterling's face. "Did you really just call me a kid? Damn, dude. I know I have a baby face, but I swear I'm grown."

German chuckled. It was a low and deadly sound, even though Jathan felt certain he didn't intend it that way. "When you get to be my age, everyone is a kid."

"So I have maybe five years left until I too am a crotchety old man, is that what you're saying? Because there's no way you're that much older than me."

"I assure you, I am." He stood. "Come on. I think I have Jathan's tastes figured out. We'll head down to the cafeteria and pick something out. He won't eat unless we make him." His light blue eyes focused on Jathan. "Cassius is still posted outside the door. Do you want me to send him in to sit with you?"

Jathan shook his head. Honestly, he looked forward to the reprieve from everyone looking at him. "I'd rather he stayed out there and keep an eye out for Quince's dad. That old bastard has been relentless for someone who doesn't really give a shit about their son."

"Performative parenting. It'll pass when Quince is out of here."

Jathan nodded. He knew that. All he had to do was look to his mom to see what a real parent looked like. She had been amazing his whole life and that hadn't changed through this. He had to make her go home. She wanted to stay and fret. But the two of them worrying together actually made things harder. He needed her handling his life outside of this room more than he needed an anxiety buddy. Like the superhero she was, his mom had everything under control, leaving him free to simply exist at Quince's side. He didn't know how much longer they had together, but he didn't want to miss a second.

"I'll be right back with some lunch for you."

Jathan nodded. He didn't watch the pair leave. His gaze returned to the wall where it stayed. He would be here to the end. No matter what that end looked like. Jathan owed Quince his life. He was welcome to it.

Chapter Nine

THERE WAS NO WAY Jathan's neck didn't hurt, sleeping at the angle he slept. Sitting next to him in a chair, with his ball cap pulled low, Jathan looked uncomfortable as hell. That couldn't be good for his injured ribs and back. He couldn't take it.

"Did they X-ray your ribs?" Quince blinked at the sound of his voice. He didn't sound like himself.

Jathan's head shot up. His gaze locked on Quince's face. His gorgeous light brown eyes almost looked crazed. He jumped to his feet. "Hey, gorgeous. You're awake."

"I notice you're not answering me."

Jathan's blinding smile was beautiful. He opened his mouth to tell him, but lost his breath.

Jathan visibly panicked. "He can't breathe. Get help, German."

Quince's head spun. He panted until everything cleared again. "Sorry. Not sure what happened there."

"Do I need to sit you up? Do you think that would help?"

Now that he said something, Quince wasn't sure why he was on his back. "Yeah. I should sit up." The more time that passed, the more confused he felt. He didn't have time to ask a single question. The coughing set in. He thought he might pass out.

Oxygen just didn't want to reach his brain. Alarms blared, making things worse. His head pounded. Then nurses stood over him. An oxygen mask covered his face. People spoke, asking him questions. He kept trying to see past them to get to Jathan. Quince didn't understand what was happening.

Jathan shoved his way in. "Hug the pillow, baby." He pushed a pillow into his arms.

Quince automatically obeyed.

"Take slow breaths."

Quince focused on breathing slower. The pillow oddly helped with the pains in his chest, but not enough. "Hurts."

Jathan rubbed his arm. "Okay. Just let these ladies work, all right? They're about to give you something to help."

He kept his gaze locked on Jathan. "Okay." Quince still wanted to panic, but Jathan was there. If Jathan was there, then everything would be fine. His struggle to breathe eased.

A nurse smiled at him. "There we go. You have to take these things slow. Don't rush. You can't pop up after a month on your back and expect to jump out of bed."

His gaze shot to Jathan. Quince's confusion doubled. He looked around the room again. Quince was definitely at Jathan's house, but the bed he was in was a hospital bed. He searched his lagging brain. The last thing he remembered was Jathan telling him he wasn't crazy for feeling so strongly about them. That he felt the same. Then... nothing.

Jathan thanked the pair of nurses.

They nodded and smiled. "We're right down the hall. It'll take time for the fluid to clear from his lungs. Just don't let him do too much too quickly."

Jathan walked them to the door. He lingered in the doorway for a moment, talking to a huge guy... German. Quince knew his name. He was Jathan's new guard. There was something missing. Something lingering just out of sight. After a few instructions and nods, Jathan was back at his side.

"Talk to me." Quince still didn't have enough breath to ask the hundreds of questions he had.

Thankfully, Jathan seemed to understand exactly how confused Quince was. "Judging by your level of panic, I'm going to assume you don't remember anything. You were shot. The bullet bounced around, doing as much damage as possible before lodging in your lung. At first, when they weren't confident you'd make it, they kept you asleep so you could heal. Then they took away that medication when it looked like you had a shot, and you didn't wake up." Jathan's voice cracked. He cleared his throat. "They wanted to move you to a rehabilitation facility for coma patients, but I refused. I knew you'd get more help with private care, so Tip signed the paperwork to get you transported here to where I hired a team. You have no fucking idea how happy I am to see your beautiful eyes again."

As insane as it likely was, Quince couldn't move past one detail. "You've been sleeping in a chair for a goddamn month." While his irritation had given him the strength to bitch, he regretted it immediately when he fell into another coughing fit. Jathan visibly fretted until it passed.

He rubbed Quince's leg. "There's no reason to get upset. No, I haven't slept here every night."

"That's a lie," German said, poking his head inside the door before disappearing again.

Irritation crossed Jathan's features, but he pressed on. "I didn't want to leave you tonight. When the doctor checked on you earlier, he said your lungs were starting to fill. I wanted to be here in case you started struggling for air."

Quince stared at Jathan and emotion swelled inside him until it got too big to hold on to. "I love you. I don't know why I feel such a huge need to get that off my chest, but I do." He coughed again. Quince was hyper aware meds held back the worst of the blinding pain. But this was too important, and Quince couldn't stop. "It's okay if you're not ready to hear that. I just need you to know it."

Jathan kissed his forehead. "I love you too." He whispered the words like that was as loud as his voice would go. "You can't leave me."

While Quince still didn't have a huge grip on how he ended up in this situation, he knew he couldn't let Jathan down. "Yeah. I'm not going anywhere. You'll be trying to peel me off you like industrial strength Velcro. *Slllrrp*." Imitating the sound of ripping away Velcro made Jathan laugh, so it was worth how hard he fought not to cough up a lung.

"You have to stop trying to talk, fucking Chatty Cathy. You sleep for a month while I beg you to wake up, then you just pop up with all the words."

He knew Jathan used humor to cover up how stressed he had likely been. That was one of the many reasons Quince couldn't stop smiling, despite his guilt. He hated that he had made Jathan worry.

"Cuddle with me and I'll be quiet."

Jathan eyed the tiny bed. "Are you sure? You're supposed to be healing here."

Quince fought to scoot over a little. He shook from the effort.

Jathan let down the railing. "For fuck's sake. Stop straining. I'll squeeze in."

"You can do it. Everyone has room for a Twizzler."

He heard a bark of laughter from the hallway. Damn. Apparently, Jathan had let these security guys get comfortable. He wasn't surprised. Jathan was too fucking nice. That was why he needed security in the first... the memory slammed into him. Quince saw that kid's face all over again. His chest ached for a different reason. He was so young.

Quince made it until he had Jathan in his arms. "What happened to the kid?" No matter how hard he tried, he couldn't speak that question above a whisper.

Jathan stroked his stomach and stared at nothing, as if only seeing the images inside his head. "Steven shot him in the leg, and then German tackled him. He's okay. They admitted him into a mental health facility."

"He couldn't help it. I saw that in his eyes. When I went down, I saw his face. He didn't know how to stop."

He watched Jathan swallow. The pain in his expression was killing Quince. "I thought you said you'd rest if I snuggled with you."

"I really want to kiss you, but apparently, I really need this full-face oxygen shit." He smiled. Quince actually felt a little better. Holding Jathan was magic. "Also, I guess I haven't brushed my teeth in a month."

A bark of laughter burst from Jathan. "I'd never leave you like that. Your care team has taken care of you in every way."

"Well, that's slightly humiliating."

Jathan pulled Quince's mask away for half a second to steal a quick peck. He made sure the mask was perfect before he settled down again. "Will you rest if I tell you about my ribs?"

"Oh, fuck. I didn't ruin the finals, did I? You'd better say you still played." Getting worked up was the wrong move. He thought he would die before he stopped coughing.

Jathan looked stressed, which made him feel worse.

"Sorry."

Irritation flashed in Jathan's eyes. "Don't be sorry. Just rest."

Quince settled down, determined. He had already stolen a month from Jathan.

Jathan pulled a necklace out from beneath his shirt to show him. A championship ring hung from the chain. "I played. I knew you'd never forgive me if I didn't." He toyed with it for a second and then tucked it beneath his shirt again. "Anyhow, I have three cracked ribs. They're on the mend."

"My baby." Quince whispered the words. He was going downhill fast, but he hoped Jathan heard the pride in his voice.

He watched a tear slip from the corner of Jathan's eye. Jathan swiped it away. He sniffed. "Sorry. I was so fucking scared I had lost this. You should've never risked yourself for me."

"Shut up and sleep with me."

A sad smile touched Jathan's lips. "Okay."

Quince might have laughed if his chest didn't hurt so badly and he knew he would start coughing again. Plus, his eyelids were just too heavy. Tomorrow, he would tell Jathan all about how he would die for him any day of the week. Right now, he just wanted to hold his miracle and sleep.

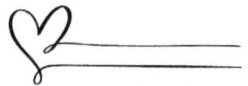

The smell of hay and horses was Sterling's aromatherapy. This barn had been more of a home to him than any house had ever been. He brushed down his final horse for the night with his mind on lockdown. His brain had always been a very dark and ugly place.

"Don't you live in Miami now?"

A smile tugged at Sterling's lips at the sound of Buck's voice. That was another part of this barn that was as familiar to him as breathing. "I still have a house here too, thankfully. If it weren't in Tip's name, Mom likely would've sold it the second she noticed I was gone."

"You're safe, then. She likely never noticed."

Ouch. Except it was true, and so it shouldn't hurt anymore. There hadn't been a single day in his life when he had been wanted. It didn't matter how much family he had on paper; Tip was his only family.

"How are you enjoying being the new foreman? The position fits you."

"It's only temporary. Quince will be back. In fact, I came out here to tell you Quince is awake. Now you have an excuse to go see that guard you have your eye on."

Sterling tossed the brush aside and focused on Buck. Damn. He was still just huge and... huge. His chest hurt. "Jealous?"

Buck snorted. "You're still the same spoiled kid who thinks everyone wants him."

If only that were true. Truthfully, he was just a fucked-up guy who saw sex as affection because absolutely no one wanted him. The worst part was he knew that about himself and didn't know how to fix it. Sex was still better than being ignored. Buck had always been way too good at ignoring him. That only made Sterling want him more. "Not everyone. That's never been true. I still have a dildo named Buck that I can't get enough of."

In a flash, Sterling found his back against the wall. Nearly three hundred pounds of solid pissed-off cowboy had him pinned. "One of these days, being a tease will get you hurt."

Sterling untucked the T-shirt Buck wore beneath his unbuttoned flannel. He held Buck's dark blue stare as his hands slipped beneath. Buck's skin was slightly damp from working in the heat all day. Sterling wanted to lick every inch.

"Quince won't choose to come back. He has Jathan now. You deserve the foreman position."

Buck didn't soften. A muscle in his jaw ticked. "Don't try to make me want things I'll never have. That's all you ever do."

Sterling couldn't help it. He wanted things he would never have. Sterling didn't know how to stop passing that pain along. He slowly drew Buck closer. Anger and hatred flashed in Buck's eyes, but he gave in—the way Sterling knew he would. His kiss was violent. That had the pains in Sterling's chest doubling. He still remembered when Buck's kisses had been filled with love and hope. Buck had treated him like precious glass, while whispering how he would marry Sterling someday. Now he bit and sucked, treating Sterling like the whore he was. He moved to Sterling's neck and Sterling's eyes burned. The urge to cry nearly brought him to his knees.

"You still smell the same." The cracked and pained-sounding whisper was out of his control.

Buck dropped his forehead to Sterling's shoulder. His body expanded so hard with each breath, it was like he had run for miles. He would shove Sterling away soon. This was the last time Buck would touch him if Sterling didn't do something.

"Tell me you hate me. It's okay. Say you don't even think about me because I make you sick. Tell me all the things I deserve to hear. It's okay." Sterling didn't know why he kept saying that. It really wasn't okay. He had never been fine.

"You're right. I hate you." He shoved himself away from Sterling and didn't look back.

Sterling's eyes closed. He kept them squeezed shut as he banged the back of his head against the wall. Maybe he hated Buck too. He couldn't tell anymore.

Everything tipped on its head and Sterling's eyes burned as he found himself over a very solid shoulder. "Fuck you for this."

Buck threw him down in a pile of hay inside a stall and slammed the door behind them. The rage in his expression had Sterling's entire body igniting. He was about to get fucked in the hard way only Buck could do. It was fine. Sterling would take Buck's hatred over anyone else's love any day. At least this was real.

Chapter Ten

THE SUN BLINDED JATHAN as he slowly came awake. Thick, cozy blankets covered him while a hard, delicious body acted as his pillow. God, he had missed the sound of Quince's heart beating against his ear. He honestly had no idea why it felt like they had been together forever. Jathan was fully attached. It was like this wasn't their first lifetime together. He couldn't imagine never having this again.

It was slow to dawn on him that he was in his bed...and so was Quince. He experienced a moment of panic that made him realize how terrified Quince had to have been when he woke up after a month of sleep.

"How are you feeling?"

Jathan lifted his head.

Quince looked a lot better.

"How are we in bed?"

A bright smile exploded across Quince's face. "Apparently, you haven't slept very well the past month. You slept all the way through German moving you to the bed. I had the nurses help me join you when you still hadn't woken after a full day. You slept almost forty-eight hours straight."

Jathan blinked. "Wow. Well, you're a good pillow."

A laugh burst from Quince. It didn't send him into a coughing fit.

"You look like you feel better."

Quince nodded. "It seems I really just needed to get upright and moving a little. I'm still coughing some, but I don't feel like I'm dying as much anymore."

Sympathy poured through Jathan. He had been through so much. "I'm so sorry. All of this is my fault."

A sweet smile touched Quince's lips. "Please don't. This is the first time in over a decade that I finally feel like I'm not a failure. I kept you safe, and I'd do it again. When I went down, I knew I was dead, and I was okay because you weren't hurt. Maybe I'm not your bodyguard, but I am your man. I kept you safe. I did my job."

Jathan heard him. He had silently blamed himself for failing Jayda all these years. It hadn't gone that way with Jathan. This experience set him free. Gave him redemption. Jathan wouldn't steal that from him. "Do you know what?"

Quince's smile grew. "What?"

"You are my man."

"Damn right." The pride in Quince's voice had Jathan grinning like a fool.

"Do you know what else?"

"What?"

"I love you."

Quince traced the line of Jathan's jaw. "I love you too. Do you know what?"

Jathan couldn't temper his happiness, no matter how hard he tried. "What?"

"I'm going to be stuck in your bed for a long time. You should see me try to walk. It's worse than a newborn horse."

Jathan sat straight up and ended up on his knees, facing Quince. "Why in the fuck are you trying to walk?"

His eyes swam with laughter. "Baby, I have to sometime. The sooner the better." He urged Jathan back into the arms. "Come on. Don't you want me to get better?"

Jathan knew he grumbled like a kid, but fuck. "I've spent a month at your side, worrying my ass off. Have some mercy on my heart. I think I've aged five years."

"Then you're five years closer to me in age."

Jathan snorted as he snuggled against Quince's side. "Nothing wrong with your age." He muttered the words under his breath, sounding childish even to his ears. Jathan felt Quince shake with laughter. His stomach suddenly growled loudly. Jathan's hand flew to his midsection. "Sorry. Dang. I guess it's been a while since I've eaten much of anything."

"Everything he's had, we've had to force down his throat."

A loud groan burst from Jathan. "Damn it, German! If you're always going to be this big of a tattletale, we're going to have problems."

"Sorry, not sorry. You're the one who has me listening at doors to make sure Quince is safe. He deserves to know you've been killing yourself like that'll solve anything."

Jesus. The guy was a busybody. Why had he let Quince talk him into hiring security? "Were you this big of a meddler when you were a bodyguard? Don't answer that. Of course you were. You're bossy as hell."

Quince huffed, making Jathan smile. He had missed their banter with every fiber of his being. "Look, sometimes celebrities have to be told to eat. You tell me why you all won't take care of yourselves."

"I'm not a celebrity."

Quince and German snorted at the same time.

Jathan growled. "If you're going to be living here, you two can't be ganging up on me all the time. It's bad for my complexion."

The silence in the room was deafening.

Jathan lifted his head again, worried he had played too much for Quince's health. He was so much larger than life. It was easy to believe he was better than he was. "Are you okay?"

Quince stared hard at Jathan—like his insides had frozen and he waited for Jathan to thaw him. "What's wrong? Do I need to get the nurse?"

Quince didn't respond.

Jathan panicked. "Grab a nurse, German."

"No." Quince spoke loud enough for German to hear. He cleared his throat. "No.

I'm good." Quince lowered his tone, keeping their conversation between them. "Do you really want me to live here?"

Jathan realized his mistake. He had gotten so used to Quince being there, he had forgotten Quince had a life outside of him. A life he probably couldn't wait to get back to. Jathan tried hard to sound normal—like his chest wasn't caving. "Sorry. I guess I forgot for a second that I can't keep you. You have a house you built specifically for yourself and whatnot. Your job is waiting. I don't know what I was thinking." Jathan rolled from the bed. He tried hard to hang on to his smiles. This whole situation with Quince sacrificing himself and Jathan taking care of him—it made things feel more intimate than they were. Jathan was more than a little embarrassed. He had warned Quince he got too attached to people. "Have you eaten? What would you like? What are the nurses saying you're cleared to eat? Never mind. I'll ask them. You'll probably try to trick me into a steak." Jathan walked away, moving faster than normal. He probably looked like he ran. "What about you, German? Have you eaten?"

"I'm good."

Jathan nodded and kept moving. He couldn't breathe. When he made it to the kitchen, out of sight, he covered his face. Jesus. What was happening to him? He pinched the spot between his eyes and took a deep breath. Quince was awake now and Jathan had slowed down enough for the stress to catch him. He stood at the kitchen counter and stared at nothing. It was okay. Things were fine. They were good. Perfect, actually. Jathan had no reason to be upset. In fact, he wasn't. Quince was on the mend. He would go home soon, and they would simply return to being a normal couple, dating. That was how this worked. He just needed a Xanax or something. Jathan had been wound tight for too long now. Too many things had been on his plate at once, wearing him down. He needed to just take a breath, eat something, and then this pressure sitting on his windpipe would go away. This was not at all a panic attack.

"Jathan."

Jathan nearly jumped out of his skin at Quince's voice. He spun. Quince was in a wheelchair. "What in the fuck are you doing out of bed?" He sounded so enraged, even he blinked at his tone. "Sorry. I don't know why that came out like that. Should you be up and moving around like this yet?" There. Adult like, but not psycho. Maybe a little breathless, but Quince had startled him.

"I'd still be in bed if you hadn't run away."

He sounded so calm. Jathan felt twice as dumb. He wanted the last ten minutes back. "Did you decide if you want something to eat?"

"I want you to talk to me."

Sitting there in his white T-shirt and red pajama pants with his hair all a mess, Quince was so beautiful and reasonable. Jathan couldn't breathe looking at him. He sucked air. Jathan literally couldn't breathe. It was like everything he had barely held at bay hit him. He bent at the waist and tried like hell to draw a single breath. Nothing happened. Only a loud, wheezing noise escaped him.

"Holy shit. German!"

In a distant sort of way, he heard feet stamping toward him. Everything went black around the edges of his vision. No matter how hard he fought, the weight on his chest wouldn't let up and his mind was in full meltdown mode. Then there was nothing.

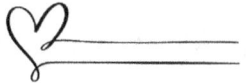

Quince couldn't sleep. Maybe he had just slept too much in the past month. Mostly, his brain wouldn't shut down. He couldn't stop staring at Jathan or running his fingers through his hair. Jathan looked so peaceful. Not at all like a man ready to be committed like this morning. Quince felt helpless. That feeling was twice as strong since he literally was useless until he regained his strength. Now they were both down, and Quince wanted to scream.

They had been so happy this morning. Then Quince had to fuck things up by pointing out what Jathan said about him living here. He had been caught off guard—more so by the immediate desperation he felt for Jathan to be serious. Quince had tried so hard to hide his hope, so Jathan wouldn't feel pressured. He didn't know what happened. Jathan just fell apart. That was on Quince in a thousand ways. Between the playoffs, finals, a stalker, and Quince almost dying while also leaving his own injuries untreated, Jathan had been doomed to eventually break down. According to German, Jathan was much worse than he pretended since Quince woke. Apparently, a guy had played extra dirty all through the finals, taking full advantage of Jathan's injuries. But Jathan had been so on autopilot, he had just played his God-given talent and won while completely checked out. He said Jathan had barely eaten and only slept in short bursts next to Quince's bed. No matter what anyone did or said, it was like he couldn't hear them. He just stayed with Quince.

Thanks to chatting with Jan, he also had more insight into the Isaac situation. It seemed Isaac was a ball boy for the team. He had easy access to Jathan right under everyone's noses. Isaac hadn't stolen the sensor from Jathan's car. It was worse than that. He had cloned Jathan's phone and had even spent some time actually living in Jathan's garage. The guy had problems, and Jathan had been the kind person that he was. It was no one's fault, really. Sometimes people's brains just turned against them. It was terrifying, actually. It was something that could happen to anyone. No one was immune. Part of Quince wanted to hate the guy, but he was barely more than a kid and that gunshot had done something to his relationship with Jathan. It was like they had been ramped up by a million degrees. The way Quince felt was almost ridiculous. He just wanted to be right here with Jathan until his heart was satisfied. Quince also needed to send that Steven guy a lifetime supply of Twizzlers. Quince hadn't realized it was armed security that guarded the neighborhood. It made sense when he thought about it. Jathan wasn't the only famous person on the block. Steven had just gotten off work but decided to make one more sweep of things. If he hadn't, there was no telling how far things would have gone. Of course, that was on German too. It seemed he was the perfect hire.

Jathan had dealt with all the things alone. Everything came at a price. Quince fucking hated this.

"I wish like hell you'd given me five minutes to say I want to be here. Or you at my place or even buying a different house together?

But yeah, wherever you sleep at night, that's where I want to be too."

"I am in so much ridiculous fucking pain right now, but *awww*."

Fuck. He was a hilarious mess. "How long have you been awake?"

"You woke me up talking." Jathan's eyes opened. He tried to stretch and gasped. Then he went right back to not breathing.

Quince grabbed the oxygen mask the nurses had left nearby just for this purpose. Another reason for Quince not to sleep. He needed to watch Jathan breathe.

"Let's get this on." He slipped it over Jathan's head and tightened it into place. "Just take slow, steady breaths. Look at me."

Jathan focused on him. He held Quince's stare without blinking.

Quince worked to keep him calm. He smiled, hoping Jathan relaxed. "You must be the luckiest person alive simply from the timing of the people you surround yourself with. The doctor had just gotten here to check on me when you collapsed. It seems you're too tall to be having panic attacks with broken ribs. Which, by the way, is much worse than you told me, so I'm not happy about that. Your lung collapsed."

"Fantastic."

Quince fought a laugh at the droll response. "They inserted a needle between your ribs. That's probably why you're in so much pain. They've got pain meds for you whenever you're ready."

"You're not supposed to be taking care of me. You're not healed yet."

Quince sighed. "Sometimes, you really piss me off, Jathan Wesley Dexter."

"Full government name. Wow. Discipline me, Daddy."

Quince dropped his head on Jathan's chest and fought not to laugh. Jathan was so awkwardly unserious. That line had been delivered with zero finesse. Jathan was just so the opposite of that joke that it was hilarious. "Fuck. You've really brightened every corner of my life and you don't even know it." He settled in, snuggling even closer. "This is forever, you know? That means we take care of each other. Even if we have to kick back, half dead together. That's the key word. We're in it together." He stroked Jathan's stomach. "We can take turns crying from the pain, if you'd like. You can go first. I've already had my meds for the night."

A wheezed laugh escaped Jathan. "You've heard me drunk. Give me pain meds and I might do or say anything."

Quince couldn't stop smiling. "I don't know. When you were drunk that one night, you acted like you might start talking dirty at any moment, asking what I was wearing. Maybe I want to see how far you'll go."

"Bring on the pain meds, then. I'm game."

"Be right back." Quince rolled from the bed and shakily transferred into the wheelchair. He wasn't helpless. Quince was just weak. He wouldn't get stronger if he didn't work at it. It didn't take him long to get a nurse. They were constantly rotating, but always ready to jump in. It took longer for Quince to maneuver the wheelchair than anything. By the time he pulled himself back into bed, Jathan had already gotten a shot.

"I asked for pills and she told me no."

The nurse laughed at Jathan's petulant tone. "One ounce of water every hour for twenty-four hours. Nothing else by mouth.

By then, we'll know if this is something that'll require surgery."

Jathan groaned. "It's the off season. This is supposed to be the boring half of my year."

Quince snuggled close again as the nurse left them alone. "Are you complaining about being stuck in bed with me?"

"Only because this isn't for a fun reason."

"I think you're fun."

At his confession, Jathan took his hand and gently squeezed. He didn't let go. "I think we should live at the ranch."

Quince hated how much hope struck him. Maybe he had ended up in the middle of nowhere from running away, but he loved the quiet. "We can always build on to my place so you don't lose your pottery studio. I mean, we need a garage for all your cars anyhow."

"This place doesn't feel the same." The softly spoken confession broke Quince's heart. Jathan needed to talk to him, though. He couldn't keep everything bottled inside. "It'll be worth the two-hour drive for games."

"Fuck. I didn't think about that. We could rent a place closer to the stadium during the season."

Silence dragged on for much longer than Quince liked. For a minute, he wondered if Jathan had fallen asleep. "I could retire."

Quince's immediate knee-jerk reaction was to say absolutely not. Jathan would not give up his dreams for this bullshit. Except this wasn't his decision, and he didn't know what went on inside Jathan's head. He chose a different approach. "I wish you'd wait on that decision until we're both on our feet."

"And I'm not high as a kite."

A smile stretched Quince's lips. "And you're not high as a kite," he agreed. "Do you need to put one foot on the floor?"

"Nah. I have you to keep me steady."

"Yeah, you do." Quince wasn't going anywhere. He was in this for life.

Chapter Eleven

THE COLD SHOWER WALL pressed against Jathan's back, steadying him. Nothing existed except the intense way Quince watched him. Those steel-gray eyes penetrated Jathan's soul as Quince rocked inside him. Everything was on fire. He wanted so badly to grab his dick and take the relief he desperately needed. But he clung to Quince's shoulders and waited on the satisfaction he knew only Quince could give him.

"I love you." Quince's voice sounded exactly like he said the only words in his head—powerful.

"I love you too."

Quince studied him—like working on a problem and then changed angles slightly.

Jathan thought his eyes would roll back in his head. He hadn't thought it could get better.

"That's it. I love watching you come. Let me see it now."

Jathan focused harder on the way Quince felt inside him. Every thrust was delectable. He didn't want to stop, but he also needed to blow. Plus, Quince's muscles had to be screaming. Jathan had given him one hell of a workout. His muscles tightened. Jathan held his breath. As badly as he wanted to close his eyes and savor every second, looking into Quince's soul was so much better.

"Yes."

At Quince's whisper, Jathan exploded. Cum shot through the air, hitting his chest. Inhuman sounds fell from his lips as his body sang with pleasure.

A strangled cry tore from Quince.

Jathan still couldn't look away. Quince was sexy as fuck when he filled Jathan with cum. Jathan had done that. He had taken Quince to the moon. It was empowering. The love he felt all hours of the day was amplified by a thousand. They were connected in a way Jathan had never been with anyone else. They were flawless. He couldn't wait to spend the rest of his life with this heart-stopping man. Quince was so beautiful.

The way he gently held Jathan, after letting his feet hit the floor, made Jathan's eyes sting. He washed Jathan and cleaned every inch of him with the gentlest care—like Jathan was precious to him. Jathan knew—of all the decisions he had made in his life—the choice to forgive Quince all those months ago was the best decision he had ever made. If Quince had never apologized. If Jathan had been stubborn. A million tiny things led them into the most dazzling life he could have never imagined for himself. This kind of happiness was for other people. Jathan had done nothing in his life to deserve this.

"You're beautiful and I never, ever want to know what's it like to wake up without you."

At his words, Quince turned twice as fierce as he had been all morning. "You'll never find out. This is until we die. You're mine."

Sometimes, he could be darkly intense. Jathan loved it. They took care of each other. By the time they turned off the water, they were squeaky clean. Jathan couldn't stop smiling or let go of Quince. He held on to his arm until he had no choice but to get dressed.

"I'll make breakfast."

Quince was way too good to him. "I'll help."

A bright smile lit Quince's face. "You absolutely will not, my beautiful disaster. Sit on the couch where your inner, feral cooking demon can't burn our food."

A snort burst from Jathan as they made their way down the hall. "Cooking demon? I'm not that bad."

Quince shot him a disbelieving look. "You burnt tea. How in the fuck does that even happen?"

Jathan shrugged. "It could happen to anyone."

"Not in under ten seconds, it doesn't. You should be in a book of records somewhere. No way that kind of destructiveness isn't legendary."

Jathan couldn't stop laughing. "I guess God had to draw the line somewhere. Otherwise, I might've turned out too perfect."

The sound of shouting cut through their laughter. They exchanged glances and headed for the door. Since moving to the ranch, it was always quiet. Any shouting outside their door couldn't be good.

Quince looked out first, keeping Jathan tucked behind him. An aggravated growl burst from him.

"For fuck's sake." He stepped outside like a man ready to fight.

Jathan peeked out the door behind him. Quince's dad, Frank, alongside an older woman, had a shotgun held on them in the yard.

"What in the hell is going on out here?"

Jathan stepped outside behind Quince, more than ready to have his back.

Buck answered over his shoulder, "I found these two wandering the ranch. They claim to know you."

The loud sigh Quince released Jathan felt in his soul. Quince sounded tired as hell. "It's my parents."

At his words, Buck lowered the shotgun, and Jathan's gaze snapped to the woman. He had always wondered why Quince's mother was never with Quince's dad. It was a sore subject, though. Jathan didn't bring it up.

"My apologies." Buck mumbled the words like he wasn't sorry at all.

"Don't apologize. You might still have to shoot them. What are you doing here?"

Quince's dad said something, but his mom spoke over him, drowning him out. "I wanted to see you."

"You've seen him. Now let's go. He's not our son anymore."

"Shut up!" His mom's shout caught Jathan so off guard, he jumped. "Shut up. Shut up. Shut the fuck up. I'm not missing my only child's wedding because of you. I've already lost too much. If you want to stay married, then shut your fucking mouth or I can let this guy shoot you."

Jathan bit his bottom lip to keep from laughing.

Quince's mom focused on him. "I'm Beth. It's really nice to meet you."

Jathan smiled. He wanted this for Quince. Jathan had a great mom. He couldn't imagine anyone living without theirs. "Jathan. It's nice to meet you too."

"Is it okay?" She motioned between Quince and herself. Her voice broke.

Jathan looked Quince's way. His jaw was locked like Jathan had never seen it. He gave his mom a jerky nod.

She stepped around Buck and rushed up the steps to hug him. Jathan had a hard time catching everything she babbled between sobs as she hugged Quince. There was a lot about Quince's dad lying to her, saying Quince hated her and didn't want to talk to her. There was also something about being in the dark. She had no idea he had been shot or was engaged or anything about his life at all until she caught his dad watching a story about them on some sports channel. He knew exactly which story she meant. It had been scheduled to be released this morning. She had to have rushed straight here. Jathan had no idea exactly what Quince's dad had been doing, but it was obvious his deep-seated prejudices didn't extend to Beth. It looked to him like she was just a mom who loved her son.

Beth swiped her cheeks and hugged Jathan before he saw it coming. "Holy hell. I thought I raised a tall son. Your dad must be a giant."

"It's his mom, actually." Quince's voice sounded dead.

Beth had the same nearly silver eyes. Jathan couldn't look away from her. She looked so sad. Beth tried to smile, but it was obvious she had a hard time holding it. "Is she a good mom? Has she been taking care of you?"

God, she broke Jathan's heart, and he hated Quince's dad even more than before.

He watched Quince visibly swallow. "She's a good person."

Beth nodded. "Would it be okay if we spent some time together?"

Quince's gaze moved towards his dad.

Beth's expression hardened. She glanced over her shoulder. "You can go. I'll call you when I'm ready to leave."

"Beth—"

She swiped her hand through the air. "I swear to God if anything other than 'yes, ma'am' comes out of your mouth right now, it'll be your last words."

Jathan's gaze slid between them. He didn't look or feel triumphant. No one won in this game. Whatever Quince's dad had done had ruined lives. Frank walked away. Jathan might have feared for Beth's safety with the bastard if it wasn't obvious the guy's fear of losing her was bigger than his hatred for Quince.

Jathan focused on Beth. "Quince was about to make breakfast. Would you like to join us?"

Beth smiled. It was sweet and lit her perfectly round face. "I'd love that."

Jathan opened the door and waved her inside. Before Jathan could follow, Quince grabbed his arm. His mouth covered Jathan's and Jathan felt the way he shook. Jathan vowed, whatever happened, he would be right there with Quince. That was where he belonged.

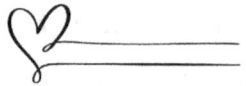

The day had been such a mixture of wonderful and bittersweet. Quince swore a haze coated his every thought for more hours than he liked. Even several hours after his mom left, he kept catching himself frozen and staring into space. His shock was so deep, he didn't know where to go with it. Quince never spoke of his mom for a reason. Losing his dad hadn't felt like that big of a deal. The guy was awful. But losing his mom had cut all the way to the bone. While he had known his mom would never leave his dad, until it happened, he had never dreamed she would cut him from her life either. Turned out, she hadn't. The lengths his dad had gone to make her believe

Quince hated her were psychotic. He had gone as far as to buy a prepaid phone to trick her into thinking Quince had changed his number to get away from her. Each time she called, it went straight to a voice mailbox with a generic message. She hadn't known where to even start looking for him, and when she tried to hire a private investigator, he had put his foot down, refusing to let her have the money to invest in a son who didn't want her. Even though it had broken her heart, she had to eventually give up for the sake of her mental health. It wasn't until she caught Frank mumbling about how Quince was dead to him while watching that interview that she got the truth. Nearly thirteen years lost, and he doubted their marriage would survive it. Quince just didn't know where to go with the overload of emotions. He hadn't known a father could hate their child so much. A therapist had once told him his dad was likely jealous of his mother's love for him. Some people couldn't stand to share their spouses, even with their child. Quince hadn't taken those words to heart at the time. After all, he hadn't spoken to his mother either. But now his entire life made sense, and he was just coasting while trying to deal.

"Tell me how to help."

Quince yanked his head from the clouds and focused on Jathan. Jathan looked sick with worry. Nothing could have broken the shock faster. "I don't guess there's anything anyone can do. What's done is done." An uncomfortable laugh escaped Quince. "So, what was it like to be raised by normal people?"

Jathan looked confused for a second. "How would I know? I don't talk to my dad either, and you've met my mom."

Quince smiled. He felt better by the second. "I have. She's wonderful."

"I mean, yeah, but she's not normal. That lady is weird as hell."

A laugh burst from Quince. Jathan was everything to him—the love of his life. His rock. Quince also hadn't understood what that truly meant until Jathan. The guy just anchored his entire existence. Without him, Quince would still be adrift and miserable.

"Thank you."

"For what?" Jathan looked genuinely confused.

"For loving me." That was the foundation of it all. Quince could sit and list all the ways Jathan made everything better, but it all boiled down to love.

"I mean, I'm kind of lazy, if that tells you anything about how easy you make it."

While wearing a huge grin, Quince shook his head. He pushed the table away from the couch with his foot and moved to the floor. He put his feet on the couch and patted the spot next to him. "Come on. I know your back hurts. You're sitting all lean-y like you do when you're miserable."

With a smile, Jathan filled the spot beside him. Side by side, with their feet on the couch and holding hands, they stared at each other.

"Are you getting excited yet?"

Quince didn't need to ask what Jathan meant. He hadn't stopped wishing time would move its ass from the moment he asked Jathan to marry him. "Are you joking? Quince Dexter has an incredible ring to it."

"If I wasn't so stoked to show you off to the world by marrying you as publicly as possible, I'd beg you to elope with me right this second."

"Realistically, we only have three more days."

Jathan nodded. "Seventy-two hours. Honestly, less than that if we start breaking it down."

They both nodded. Their gazes never wavered. "Then again, no one would have to know. We could just have the wedding as planned."

Jathan's hands rose and fell. "It could be our secret."

"It would be less stressful that way."

They kept staring, as if waiting to see who broke first. Fuck it. Quince had no pride when it came to Jathan. "I'll grab our shoes."

Jathan rolled to his knees. "I'll grab our wallets and the marriage certificate."

They had already applied. All they needed was one signature. When they were on their feet, they froze and held each other's stare again. They were really doing this. Zero shame. Their love was too big to contain. It was the forever kind of love.

Keep an eye out for the next Sporting Pride, Broken Ponies.

About the Author

CHARITY PARKERSON IS AN award-winning and multi-published author with several companies. Born with no filter from her brain to her mouth, she decided to take this odd quirk and insert it in her characters. One of her greatest loves is writing morally gray characters. You'll find them scattered throughout her hundreds of titles.

*Nine-time Readers' Favorite Award Winner

*2015 Passionate Plume Award Finalist

*2013 Reviewers' Choice Award Winner

*2012 ARRA Finalist for Favorite Paranormal Romance

*Five-time winner of The Mistress of the Darkpath

Connect with her online:

*Sign up for her newsletter: https://bit.ly/charityparkersonnewsletter

*Join her readers' group on Facebook: http://bit.ly/CharitysTribe

* W e b s i t e : https://www.charityparkerson.com

*A list of her social media accounts and giveaways all in one place: http://hy.page/charityparkerson